Affection

for the

Doctor

Book Three

Small Town Matchmaker

Cheryl Wright

Affection for the Doctor
(Book Three, Small Town Matchmaker)

Copyright 2023 by Cheryl Wright

Small Town Romance Publications

Dedication

To Margaret Tanner, my very dear friend and fellow author, for her enduring encouragement and friendship.

To Alan, my husband of over forty-eight years, who has been a relentless supporter of my writing and dreams for many years.

To You, my wonderful readers, who encourage me to continue writing these stories. It is such a joy knowing so many of you enjoy reading my stories as much as I love writing them for you.

Table of Contents

Chapter One

The pounding on the door startled Marcus Ryan awake.

He glanced about—it was barely light. Dawn had arrived not long ago. Marcus grabbed his robe and slipped his slippers on his bare feet. It was undecidedly chilly at this hour of the day. Running a hand through his no doubt unkempt hair, he headed toward the front door, lighting a lantern as he went.

"Coming," he called, knowing whoever was out there was having some kind of medical emergency. Breathless from hurrying, he pulled the door open. "James!" he said, addressing the rancher he rarely saw in town. "What's happened?" The other man appeared to be in perfect condition, but one never really knew until an examination was performed.

"Sorry to wake you so early, Doc," James said in a rush. "I have my boy with me. Might be a broken arm."

Marcus held the lantern higher and further out the door. He winced as he noticed the young child sitting in the buggy, pain written all over his face. "Should I get him now?" James's voice held that of a scared parent. He was not the calm and confident man Marcus had dealt with in the past.

"I'll help," Marcus said. "If it is broken, we don't want to cause more injury." They walked to the buggy together, and he put the lantern on the floor of the buggy, then held the boy's arm carefully and gently. "Lift him down as slowly as you can. William," he said, turning his attention to the young boy, "keep as still as possible and let us do all the work."

"Yes, Sir," William said bravely, despite the pain Marcus knew he was in.

Between them, the men got the six-year-old into the doctor's office and onto the examination table.

"When did this happen?" Marcus asked as he examined the child's arm. William winced. "I'm sorry, Will," he said reassuringly. "It will be over soon." The boy put on a brave face, but tears danced in his eyes.

James sighed. "Apparently, he did it yesterday, but said nothing. I heard him crying early this morning. A simple fall from the porch, he told me."

Marcus felt for James. He'd become a widower shortly after his daughter Pearl was born. That was… he had to think. It must be four years. His wife had recovered from childbirth but contracted pneumonia some time later, leaving James with the two young ones to rear alone. "It's definitely broken." He turned and retrieved a splint from an overhead cupboard, along with several bandages.

"I'll need you to hold Will down while I set the bone," he told the boy's father, then turned to the child. "Drink this," he said, dispensing a dose of laudanum to the boy. "I'm sorry, Will. This is going to hurt a bit, but the medicine will make it less painful." He explained what he was about to do, and Will nodded. If he didn't know better, Marcus would think the boy was far older.

Marcus knew William would be in excruciating pain, but there was little he could do. James held the splint steady while Marcus bandaged it. He really could do with a nurse to help, but that was not an option. Most women didn't like to be this far away from the big city.

When he finished, Marcus glanced at the injured child. Not once did Will cry out, nor did tears fill his eyes. It wasn't normal for a child to behave that way under such duress. Perhaps he was in shock.

He listened to the boy's chest and looked into his eyes. "Do you know what day it is, Will?" he asked.

"It's Friday," the boy said. "Two more days until church."

Marcus raised his eyes to James. Will was correct. "You can sit up now," he said as he ruffled the boy's hair. "Make sure he has two drops of the laudanum twice a day if he's in pain, three times a day only if necessary. Bring him back in a week."

"Thank you, Doctor Ryan," James said, and his son repeated his thanks too.

Marcus was certain the fact Will was raised by cowboys was the reason the child was so mature, but it wasn't necessarily the best thing for him. A six-year-old needed to be allowed to be a child, not act like an adult. "Where's Pearl?" Now the emergency was past, Marcus realized James's daughter was not there.

"Asleep. My foreman is looking out for her. I really had no choice," he whispered. "I didn't want to wake her at this ungodly hour. Heck, I didn't want to wake you this early."

Marcus lifted the boy carefully from the examination table. "No running around, Will. And no jumping or riding."

"Aw, Doc," Will said. "You know I like to ride."

"You heard the doc," James said firmly. "I promise he'll take it easy," his father said, then reached a hand out to Marcus.

"I'll check that arm in a week. Any problems, don't hesitate to come back." He walked to the front door with the pair and watched as they drove away. It was then he realized he was still in his robe and slippers.

After the morning he'd already had, Marcus didn't feel like making breakfast. He quickly dressed, intending to head to the bakery. Joel would have some pastries baked by now, he was certain. The bonus was that since Molly had been working at the bakery the coffee was drinkable. At least that's what he'd heard.

He pulled on his boots and headed outside. He didn't have any patients for another hour, so he had time to linger. After the stress of the morning, Marcus needed that. It wouldn't be so bad if the patient had been an adult, but a child who showed almost no emotion? That had been nerve-wracking. Especially since he couldn't tell how much pain the boy was in.

James was a good parent—he would ensure Will was fine, and if he wasn't, he'd bring him back. Both before and after his wife died, his family had always come first. For Marcus, there was no choice. He had no family, and no one to worry about.

When he'd been offered this posting so far from civilization, he took it because he was the only one left in his entire family. Otherwise, he would have rejected it out of hand. Crystal Springs was a blip on the map. It was so small it had been difficult for him to even locate.

The offer of free lodging and an attractive stipend had appealed to him. It meant all he had to do was turn up each day and do what he'd been taught to do—fix people.

Still, there were days he wished he had help. He was certain the mayor wouldn't provide a nurse. That would cost money. Marcus was so convinced he refused to even broach the subject. He certainly could have used a trained professional this morning. Someone who knew exactly what she was doing.

Instead of pondering *what ifs,* he strolled to the bakery and opened the door. The aroma of freshly baked pastries hit him as he stood at the door. "Good morning, Doctor Ryan," Molly said cheerfully. "What can I do for you today?"

It wasn't often he went there this early. But he also wasn't usually awoken with a medical crisis this time of day. Coffee. Strong and black." Marcus sat down at one of the tables and ran his hands through his hair. Surely, his day could only get better.

Chapter Two

Molly stared at the doctor. She'd seen Marcus Ryan around, but never had much to do with him. Mostly because she was not a sickly person. That was pure luck, if she thought about it. "Is everything alright, Doctor Ryan? You look rather…stressed."

His head shot up, and he studied her. It was as though he was seeing her for the first time. Molly was used to it. She wasn't beautiful like some of the women in town, and she was fully aware of the fact. She secretly believed it to be the reason her mother sent her for all those courses—the ones that were supposed to turn her into a refined lady. But for what? No one here in Crystal Springs was interested in plain Molly Cavendish.

Her mother might put on airs, and Molly might have been taught about deportment and acting like a genuine lady, but that was as far as it went. The position she held her here at the bakery had taught her more than any of those expensive courses her mother forced her to undertake.

"I had an early start," he said, his eyes telling the story well before his words did. "Emergency."

Molly gasped. "I hope everything is alright now?" She reached for a mug and poured the coffee. It was obvious Doctor Ryan needed coffee. She placed it on the table in front of him, along with sugar and cream. "Is there anything else I can get for you?" She hovered. Molly never hovered, but for some reason she couldn't put her finger on, she felt compelled to stay. "There are fresh pastries, not long out of the oven. Joel bakes them fresh every morning."

It was true. There was never anything left over at the end of the day. Joel was an excellent baker and everyone knew it. He'd even increased the amount he made each day and the supplies were still depleted. It was a good thing, she knew it was. Joel wasn't a greedy man. It wasn't about the money for him; it was about giving people what they wanted.

She'd heard Doctor Marcus Ryan was a good man, too. Molly had little to do with him. "This is excellent coffee," he said, then took another mouthful. "What do you recommend?" he said, and stared up at her.

Recommend? Oh, the pastries. She opened her mouth to speak, but wasn't sure what to tell him. "Everything is wonderful. Joel is the best."

The doctor grinned. "So I've heard. Surprise me." She stared. She'd been taught a lady never stares, but she couldn't help herself. He was the most handsome man she'd ever met, and there were some very handsome men in Crystal Springs. Most of them married. Not that Molly wanted to marry. She might verge on being a spinster, but marriage was not on the cards for her. She was happy doing exactly what she did right now—working for Joel. She came in early and left early, then had the rest of the day to herself. Joel was a terrific boss. Not that she'd worked anywhere else to compare him.

"Are you alright?" the doctor's voice cut through her woolgathering.

She glanced down at him. "I apologize. My mind was elsewhere." She turned on her heels and headed to the pastry display cabinet. She watched him as she found two of what she considered the best. Not that it was a straightforward choice—they were all good.

She served them on a luncheon plate, along with a pristine white napkin. Nothing but the best for Joel's customers. After placing the pastries in front of him, Molly swept up his mug. She returned a short time later with it refilled.

"These are delicious," Marcus said, wiping the crumbs from his mouth.

It was then Molly did something she'd never done before. She slid down into the chair opposite him. What compelled her to do that? She honestly didn't know. She never mingled with the customers. Not ever. She served them and then went back to her post behind the counter.

She smiled across at him. "Anything Joel bakes is delicious," she said quietly, as though she didn't want Joel to hear. The truth was, he was busy in the kitchen baking more delicious goodies. He was happy there. And she was happy out here.

"Thank you," Marcus said as he observed her. "Have we met before? I don't recall," he said, still studying her. He looked a little more relaxed now.

"I've never been a patient, if that's what you mean," she said, then remembered to sit straighter in the chair. Thankfully, Mother was not about. "Until I worked here, I didn't come to town much."

"Huh," he said, then went back to his pastries. Molly took that as her cue to leave. As she stood, he glanced up at her. "Don't go. Unless…that is, unless you have to. I would hate for Joel to get cranky."

That made her laugh. Joel never got cross or irritated. Joel was always happy. Since he married Martha anyway. The twins kept them both busy, and despite being constantly on the move, those babies were everything to the pair.

Suddenly, his hand went up, and a finger caressed her cheek. Her eyes opened wide in astonishment. "Oh, I do apologize," Marcus said. "That was wrong of me." He suddenly pulled his hand away, and Molly's heart felt hollow.

She had never been courted, never kissed, never touched by a man. Perhaps that was the reason she'd felt the way she had? No matter the reason, Molly liked the way Doctor Ryan made her feel. *Is that what it feels like to fall in love?*

She shook herself mentally. Right now, she was acting like a silly teenager. "I need to get back to work," she said without further thought. "Joel will be bringing out more pastries at any moment." She stood then, and Marcus glanced up at her. His eyes watched her every move.

"It was nice chatting with you," he said. "Perhaps we can do it again sometime."

Did that mean…no. It didn't. Why would the town doctor be interested in the likes of her? A store attendant who dished out pastries and coffee. It made no sense, and she wouldn't even contemplate such a notion.

"Coming through!" Joel's voice heralded his appearance in the store. He carried a large tray of freshly baked pastries. Molly wondered why she wasn't as big as the side of a house. Joel allowed her to eat whatever her heart desired. Right now, what she desired was out of her reach.

Chapter Three

Marcus finished his pastries and second mug of coffee, then was ready to go back home. After paying Molly, he left the bakery. Joel sure was good at what he did. Perhaps he should visit the bakery more often.

He shook his head emphatically. The reason he wanted to go back was obvious, and he was having none of it. Women were a complication, and he didn't need complications in his life. He was better off sticking to medicine.

Molly was nice. Her mother, not so much. He'd only dealt with her once or twice, but she was pushy. She wasn't horrid. It was just that she liked to get her own way. He didn't like bossy women.

It made him wonder if Molly was like that, too. So far, he'd seen no sign of that behavior from her, but one really never knew.

Pastries were not the healthiest food to have for the most important meal of the day, but he felt satisfied. Whether it was the pastries or the company, he wasn't certain, but felt the latter was probably true.

He unlocked the front door to his residence and went inside, then unlocked the door to the waiting room, and headed back to the residence. If any patients arrived early, at least they could sit down and wait in comfort.

"Molly." He said her name out loud in the quiet of his home, uncertain why he did. "Molly Ryan." The name rolled off his lips as though he'd said it a thousand times before. Marcus slumped into one of the kitchen chairs in his path. He put his head to his hands. "What is wrong with you?" he yelled into the room. "She is not your wife, and never will be!"

Then it hit him. Lack of sleep. That's why he was behaving this way. He'd lost far more than an hour's sleep this morning. Not that he blamed his young patient. It was his own fault he hadn't gone to bed early enough, not young William's. Nor was it James.

Working on patient files when he should be in bed was poor form. He constantly told his patients to get sufficient sleep but didn't listen to his own advice.

Marcus checked his pocket watch. It was almost time to open. He rushed into the bathroom and freshened up. He hadn't time to trim his beard today and studied it in the mirror. It would do. His eyes were slightly red from lack of sleep. He splashed cold water on his face and they looked slightly better. Not enough to completely hide the redness, but enough to shock him awake. Marcus straightened his tie and pulled his jacket a little tighter.

Now he was presentable. Wasn't he?

He could hear movement in the waiting area. Having the surgery attached to the house was convenient, but sometimes too convenient. He checked the time again. Ten minutes before he was due to open. Only a few patients were booked in today, but there were always walk-ins—people who didn't know they'd need a doctor, or accidents that needed immediate treatment. Like this morning.

He unlocked the door that adjoined the residence and stared at the one person sitting in the waiting room. Molly. Was he dreaming? Surely Molly wasn't ill. He'd seen her only a short time ago.

"Molly." He said her name as though it was not unusual for him to utter it.

She stood and reached out a hand. "You left your wallet behind," she said, then turned to go.

Oh. "Thank you. I would have eventually searched everywhere for it."

"You need to be more careful, Doc," she said, then giggled. The sound rang out across the otherwise empty room and settled into his heart.

He stared after her, but she was no longer there. Marcus did not know how or why, but Molly had gotten under his skin. If he didn't know better, he'd swear they'd known each other for years. The truth never lied—they'd met less than an hour ago, and now his life was changed forever.

A shiver went through him. How could a chance meeting be life changing? Surely that couldn't be true? He'd heard about fate, but not once had he believed it.

"Morning, Doc."

He needed to stop woolgathering and get to work. Old man Hudson needed his attention. "Good morning, Mr. Hudson. Come through," he said, holding the door open. As he examined the old man's leg, he heard a movement in the waiting room, and knew he was in for a busy morning.

Just as well. He needed to keep his mind on his patients and not Molly Cavendish.

As predicted, the morning was a busy one. Marcus felt like it would never end. The moment the thought entered his head, he regretted it. People needed his help—it was as simple as that. He'd trained for years to have this privilege. It was an honor denied to many.

Marcus knew he had a gift, just as his father had, and his father before him. It was in his blood to help people, and from a young age, he knew he wanted to be a doctor. He'd watched his father fix endless people over the years, and knew it was his life calling. What he hadn't realized was it would mean loneliness.

His parents met before his father had trained as a doctor—and ideally, that's what Marcus should have done. Sought a wife before he'd trained. Then he might have been married by now. Perhaps even have a young family.

What was wrong with him? Staring into the face of a beauty such as Molly had sent him crazy. He'd treated many female patients but had never become irrational like this. It wasn't even as though he knew her, because he didn't.

The family lived out of town, not miles away, but on the outskirts of Crystal Springs, if he recalled correctly. He'd been there once, some years ago, when Molly's grandmother had a terrible fall. She'd since passed on. Not because of the fall, but from old age.

He liked it here in Crystal Falls. It was relatively quiet, and he had a steady stream of patients. Not that he wished anyone ill, but keeping busy was always a good thing.

This was getting him nowhere. A stroll in the fresh air. That's what he needed to get his mind back on track. He had two hours before the next patient, so a brisk walk and then something to eat would do him good.

He pulled on his hat and buttoned up his coat. Always when going from warm to cold, you should ensure you keep the heat in. At least, that was his belief. Besides, he didn't wish to appear untidy.

Marcus ran a hand through his hair. Perhaps he should visit the barber—he was looking a little scruffy.

Oh, for goodness' sake! Since when did he care if his hair was a little disheveled? Since he'd met Molly, that's when. Marcus stormed out of the house and locked the door. He really needed the fresh air.

He hadn't been gone long when he slammed into something. Or someone. "Joel!" he said, as the other man found his balance. "I apologize. Are you alright?"

Joel stared at the bag now sitting on the ground. "I am, but I'm not sure about these." He pointed, then picked up the large bag. "Pastries for the Ladies Auxiliary." He opened the bag and peeked inside. "They seem to be in one piece. Where were you going in such a rush?"

"Nowhere in particular. I needed fresh air."

Joel studied him. "My store assistant has been like that today. Must be something in the air." He glanced into the bakery through the glass window. "Wait. Molly said you came in this morning. Don't tell me…" He stopped then, and Marcus felt heat rise in his cheeks.

He feigned innocence. "Don't tell you what?" he asked, as though nothing was amiss.

"Hmmm. Well, I'd best be on my way," Joel said, and then he was gone, leaving Marcus to ponder Joel's words. Did that mean Molly was as unsettled about meeting him as he was her? He shook his head. That was ridiculous. He glanced through the glass, just as Joel had done. Molly stood behind the counter rearranging the pastries. As though she only now noticed him there, she lifted a hand and waved. Her smile brightened his day.

"Move on," Marcus told himself firmly, and hurried along the street. He would have to avoid the bakery from now on. His world had tilted earlier today, and he needed to straighten it up again.

Chapter Four

Molly's heart fluttered. She'd glanced up when she felt eyes on her. It was the doctor—he'd been out there talking to Joel. She had hardly recognized him with his hat on. He'd not worn it earlier this morning. He had been anxious and upset when he'd arrived.

Doctor Ryan didn't divulge any information about his patient or the emergency he'd faced, but it was obvious he cared about his patients. She liked that in a person. She waved, but he turned away. Molly wasn't sure if he'd noticed her waving or whether he chose to ignore her. She doubted it was the latter. He wouldn't be so rude as to do something like that. Would he?

He must be in a hurry. Almost knocking Joel to the ground had proven that. She shrugged her shoulders and got back to work. It wasn't long before the bell over the door tinkled. Molly glanced up. "Good afternoon, Mrs. Hargreaves," she said, grateful for the distraction. "What can I do for you today?"

The older woman ran an eye across the pastries carefully displayed in front of her. "I'm having some friends over this evening," she said, continuing to glance at the pastries. "Should I get all the same, or get a mixture?" She tapped her chin, and Molly realized she was talking to herself rather than to Molly. Then she glanced up. "What do *you* think, young lady?"

"I would take a mix. That way, your guests would have choices." She reached to the cupboard behind her and pulled out a large box, ready to add the delicacies. "How many were you thinking, Mrs. Hargraves?"

"At least a dozen. Mr. Hargraves will be most upset if he doesn't get his share." She grinned then—a rare thing with this customer.

Molly ran her eyes over the pastries. "Your question is answered. There aren't more than six of any of these pastries. This late in the day, there's never a lot of choice."

Mrs. Hargraves straightened. "Then Mr. Evans needs to bake more!" she said, then harrumphed.

What could Molly say to that? Joel had already increased his production, now that he didn't have to look after the store and bake. He constantly told Molly how her presence made his life far easier. It was ingratiating, to say the least. "Would you like me to make up a box of mixed pastries for you, Mrs.

Hargraves?" she asked. No point continuing the discussion. It would get her nowhere.

"Thank you, Molly. Make it fourteen, and that will hopefully be enough." Her eyes wandered to the only carrot cake left in the store. "I'll take that as well," she said, pointing in the cake's direction. It made Molly wonder how many visitors Mrs. Hargraves was having that night.

The other woman reached into her reticule and pulled out a bank note while Molly finished wrapping her purchases. "Thank you for your business," she said, handing over the packages in a large brown paper back. "Would you like me to carry these to your buggy?"

"Thank you, dear, but I'll be fine." The customer turned to leave, almost dropping her purchases in the process.

"Do let me assist you," Molly insisted, taking the bag from her. If the purchases were damaged, this difficult customer may blame her, and that would never do.

They stepped out of the store and almost ran into Marcus. Molly's heart fluttered.

"Doctor Ryan," Mrs. Hargraves said. "How lovely to see you. Out for a stroll, are you?"

The doctor's gaze moved from Mrs. Hargraves to Molly. He smiled tentatively. Molly wasn't sure if the smile was meant for her, or the older woman. "I am indeed. Time to return to my patients now though," he said and tipped his hat to the two women. In a matter of moments, Marcus was out of sight.

"A lovely young man, that one," the older woman said. "Needs to find himself a wife, though." Then she glanced at Molly. "It's past time you married, my girl." She climbed up into the buggy and Molly handed up her purchases, wishing the woman would leave. It wasn't enough her mother was constantly on her back to marry, now she had an ally.

Then it hit Molly. Mrs. Hargraves was friends with her mother. Had the two conspired to marry her off? Mother had mentioned getting Dennis Andrews involved. The self-appointed town matchmaker who caused more problems than he fixed.

Mrs. Hargraves flicked the reins and was soon gone. Molly stood staring after her for a few minutes, almost mesmerized by the dilemma she faced. She loved her job at the bakery, and didn't want to leave. She didn't particularly want to marry either. Not unless the right man came along.

She liked the doctor, but they'd met only the once. The second time didn't really count since she only returned his wallet and saw him for less than two minutes. Even then, her heart had fluttered in his presence.

What was that about?

"Molly, can you run to the mercantile and fill this short list for me?" Joel had been back for a while but startled her with his words. He handed a piece of paper to her and waved her out the door. Joel had sworn off Dennis since he'd interfered in his courtship with Martha, and refused to go into the store. After all this time, she thought he would have cooled off. Instead, he was still mad at the interfering matchmaker.

She fully understood—the man could be a nuisance. On the other hand, he had helped to get some couples together. Beth and Wyatt, for instance. Without Dennis involved, they probably wouldn't be married right now.

She wondered if Dennis thought she and Doctor Ryan were a good match. As she reached for the door handle, Molly checked herself. What was she doing? She only met the doctor this morning. He had given no sign he was interested in her.

He was handsome. She would give him that. Doctor Ryan was also hardworking. She'd been told so many times over the years, and if today was any indication, people were right. Living in that big house by himself was sad, really. The doctor's residence had been built with a family in mind, not a single man with no family. She wondered how he felt living there alone.

If it was her, Molly was certain she would feel lonely. Even living in her parent's home, she felt lonely at times. She was rarely alone there, but alone was different to lonely. She'd learned that a long time ago.

Since she began working for Joel, Molly had considered finding somewhere in town to live. That way she would be closer to work, and not have to awaken so early. Not that she was terribly far from town. Even so, it would be nice, particularly in the winter, to stay snuggled up in bed a little longer.

She pushed the thought away as quickly as it came to mind. How frightening would it be living in town by herself? The downsides of living in town—living alone, drunken cowboys running around at night— outweighed the good sides. She wanted to be an independent young woman, but she was far too scared to make it happen.

It would take a far larger leap of faith than she was prepared for.

Molly pushed open the door to the mercantile and headed toward the front counter and Dennis Andrews. "Good afternoon, Miss Cavendish," he said, a smirk on his face. "I hear you're being courted by our Doctor Ryan."

Molly glared at him. Is this the reason Joel sent her to the mercantile? To find out for herself what Dennis was really like?

Pre-warned was pre-armed. She would keep away from Dennis as much as possible. That probably also meant keeping away from Marcus Ryan. Her heart shattered at the mere thought of it.

Chapter Five

"Take these pills twice a day with water, Mrs. Hodgkins," Marcus told his patient. "Come back in two weeks and we'll review how things are going." He stood then, indicating the visit was over.

"Thank you, Doctor Ryan," the elderly woman said, and headed toward the door. She left without another word.

Marcus glanced across the waiting room and was surprised to see Molly sitting there. Was she ill? His heart fluttered. She looked perfectly fine on the three occasions he'd seen her already today. Although, to be fair, he'd only seen her through the glass the last time.

"Mr. Pickins, do you mind if I take Miss Cavendish in next?"

The patient had already begun to stand, but sat down again. "Not at all, Doctor," he said wearily. "I have nothing else to do."

"Thank you. Please come in, Miss Cavendish." He indicated for Molly to enter his office, then closed the door behind her. As he sat behind his desk, he studied her. His patient, assuming that was why she was here, appeared distraught. It was the total opposite of how she'd been every other time he'd seen her.

She opened her mouth to speak, then promptly closed it again. Molly screwed up her face as though in an effort not to cry. He'd seen it many times before with his female patients. They'd been brought up to believe crying was a bad thing, when in fact, it was good to get feelings out in the open.

"You seem upset, Molly," he said, then came around to her side of the desk and sat on the edge. "Is everything alright?" Marcus lifted her hand and comforted her. It didn't take a genius to see something awful had happened to upset her. Molly Cavendish had gotten under his skin and into his heart way too quickly. He wanted nothing more than to pull her into his arms and comfort her.

"It's Dennis," she said, appearing to blink back tears.

Marcus rolled his eyes. "What has he done now?" The entire town was over Dennis and his interfering ways. They all wished he would sell the mercantile and leave them alone.

"He…" She glanced up, tears pooling in her eyes. "He says we are courting. I don't know who else he's said it to."

Marcus had no intention of letting Dennis get him riled. "Pay him no attention," he said, but knew for someone like Molly, it was not so simple. She had a reputation to be upheld, and Dennis had suddenly put that in doubt. "I'll talk with him."

Molly nodded, then quietly stood.

It was totally inappropriate, he knew, but Marcus couldn't help himself. He stepped forward and pulled Molly into his arms. "Please don't worry," he whispered. "Dennis is a fool who needs to stop interfering in people's lives."

He handed her a clean handkerchief. "Do you need this?"

She stared at him momentarily, then shook her head. Marcus couldn't help but feel sorry for her. Molly left the room without another word.

"Mr. Pickins," Marcus said. "Thank you for waiting." His attention was not fully on his next patient, but on Molly as she left the waiting room.

"Dennis," Marcus said firmly. It was much later in the day when he'd seen all his patients. "This nonsense has got to stop."

The mercantile owner gazed at him innocently. "Nonsense, Doctor Ryan? What nonsense?"

If Marcus didn't know better, he would believe the man did not know what he was talking about. "You know exactly what I mean. Miss Cavendish is quite upset. I hope you haven't been spreading rumors around town. I might have to speak to the sheriff— let him sort it out."

Dennis stared then, his look incredulous. "But, I…" For once, the man was lost for words.

"Slander," Marcus said firmly, "is not acceptable. I'm sure Sheriff Garrett will be interested in hearing about this."

He turned to leave, certain the message had gotten through. Finally.

"Doc!" Dennis called as Marcus opened the door, his movements stiff as his anger threatened to overtake him. He didn't care what Dennis said about him, but Molly? That was a whole different situation. He would not have her reputation sullied for another man's enjoyment.

He turned to face Dennis. "What?" Marcus demanded, still furious at the storekeeper. "Haven't you done enough damage?"

Dennis studied him. Did the man think he was joking? He was prepared to storm into the sheriff's office the very minute he left the mercantile. "I'm sorry, Doc. I didn't mean to upset Miss Cavendish."

"Too late for sorry. We have never courted, and the only time I've seen her is at the bakery, and in a professional capacity." He turned away again, then spun back toward the matchmaker. "You need to mind your own business, Dennis. Keep out of mine. And especially keep out of Molly's." He couldn't be more angry if he tried. Luckily, he'd seen all his patients for the day. Marcus wasn't sure he could deal with anyone else today. Not after his encounter with the so-called town matchmaker. The man who messed up relationships rather than bringing people together.

He strode toward home. Marcus needed supplies, but had no intention of purchasing supplies from Dennis today. He couldn't bear to even look at the man, let alone allow him to profit from his purchases there.

Marcus stood outside the bakery, trying to decide what to do. At this time of day, the bakery was closed, so that was out of the question. Besides, twice in one day probably wasn't a good look. The other option was to go to the diner—it had been a long time since he'd been there for a meal.

He glanced through the glass of the bakery. Molly was long gone, and Joel likely was too. Gone home to his family. Some days, Marcus longed for a wife and children to go home to. Other days, he wondered if it was fair to even wish for such a thing. Long hours and occasional house calls in the middle of the night. Even situations like today when he was awoken in the early hours of the morning.

He shook himself mentally. Until meeting Molly, he'd never entertained such thoughts. It was ridiculous he was doing so now. Marcus turned on his heels and headed back toward the diner. He could hear laughter coming from inside before he'd even opened the door. Dining alone wasn't his most favorite thing to do, but he had little choice.

"Doctor Ryan, good evening," Allie said. "Welcome. Table for one?"

He glanced across the room. The diner wasn't full by any standards, but there were more customers than he'd imagined. His eyes continued to stroll around the room when he spotted a familiar face. Molly smiled and beckoned for him to join them. He shook his head no. Molly's parents surely wouldn't want his intrusion.

Suddenly, her father stood. "Doc, join us," he called across the room. That put him in a precarious situation. If he refused, he would appear rude. If he accepted, it would only add fuel to the fire Dennis had already started.

All eyes turned toward him. He was now in an untenable position. He really had no choice but to accept. He stepped toward the Cavendish table. "Thank you," he said. "If you are certain?"

"Of course," Joseph Cavendish said, extending his hand. "You know my wife Mildred, and I believe you've met our daughter, Molly." Joseph pulled out a chair for him.

"I met Molly for the first time this morning. At the bakery," he added in case her father had other ideas.

"Yes, Molly told me." He frowned then. "Dennis seems to have other ideas."

Marcus sighed. "I've had words with Dennis. As a matter of fact, I've not long left. There was mention of slander," Marcus said, not sure what kind of reception his words would get.

"Excellent," Joseph Cavendish said, rubbing his hands together. "The man is a nuisance."

"He certainly is," Mildred said. "He has a nerve and needs to be stopped."

Molly looked far from comfortable during the exchange. "Have you ordered yet?" Marcus asked, trying to change the subject for Molly's sake.

"We have not," Joseph told him. "We've not long arrived ourselves." He lifted a hand and waved for menus to be brought to their table. Marcus was relieved to see Molly appearing far more relaxed now.

"The food is always good here," Joseph said as he gazed over the menu. "Ah, roasted stuffed goose is on the menu tonight. They do it so well here. Anyone else up for such a delicacy?"

Everyone agreed to the same dish. Marcus settled in for an evening of good company. Including Molly.

Chapter Six

Molly shuddered when her father stood, then invited Marcus Ryan to join them for supper. He wasn't always this amiable and was sometimes the opposite. It got Molly to wondering—was her father trying to marry her off?

Surely not. Although, on second thought, she was approaching spinsterhood. Her father had ensured he was aware of the fact, and told her in no uncertain terms, it was past time to marry.

Her older sister had flown the coop years before and was happily married to her childhood sweetheart. No such luck for Molly. It was the reason her mother had sent her to deportment school. Not that it had helped in the marrying stakes.

Nor was she in a hurry to tie the knot. Not with Marcus Ryan, or any other eligible man. She was happily living as a single woman, earning her own money. It was liberating, and Molly wasn't sure she wanted to give that up anytime soon.

She also wasn't convinced Joel would be impressed if she up and left him. Their relationship as boss and employee had worked well. He had some strange habits, but once she had gotten used to them, she settled in well.

"Isn't that right, Molly?" Her head shot up at the use of her name. What were they talking about? She'd been woolgathering and not invested in the conversation one little bit.

Her father glared at her fleetingly. It was there and gone in an instant. Those who didn't know him would miss it completely. "I'm sorry, Father. My mind was elsewhere."

"I was telling Doctor Marcus what a hard worker you are." Father studied her. He was a good man, but didn't like it when she was inattentive. Especially when company was involved.

She glanced at Marcus. His expression was one of sympathy. "I have first-hand knowledge," he said. "Molly served me at the bakery this morning."

"Is that so?" her father asked, suddenly interested.

Marcus studied her. Was he trying to gauge the depth of her father's interest? "I had an early morning emergency. I was exhausted and hungry. Molly fixed both those problems." He smiled at her then, and a shiver went down her spine. If she wasn't careful, Molly could find herself completely enamored with the town doctor. "She also returned my wallet when I carelessly left it behind."

"Our Molly is a good girl," Father said, pride in his voice.

"Always has been," Mother said, not to be left out of the conversation. "We should probably order dessert now," she added, now they'd all finished the first course.

Molly wanted to crawl under the table in embarrassment.

Mother waved to the waitress to join them. Her father took charge once she arrived. "What is on the dessert menu this evening?" he asked, sounding very formal.

"We have peach cobbler, and a customer favorite, raspberry summer pudding. It's rather sweet, but light. We serve it with clotted cream."

"Who wants what?" Father asked, and once their orders were confirmed, the waitress left them alone.

"I've had a wonderful evening," Marcus said, his gaze not leaving Molly. "Not that I come here often, but when I do, I normally dine alone."

"Well, Doc," Father said firmly. "We can't have that. An upstanding and hardworking man such as yourself should never have to dine alone." Her father glanced across at Molly, then back to Marcus. "You can dine with us whenever you wish."

Molly groaned inwardly. Could her father be any more obvious? There was no way Marcus didn't see the writing on the wall. Not only was Dennis Andrews trying to match them up, but now her father had to get in on the act. She turned to Mother, her eyes pleading, but instead of sympathy, her mother was beaming.

It was apparent both her parents would welcome a successful doctor into the family. With open arms, no less.

Before anyone had a chance to comment on the last bombshell, the desserts arrived and were distributed. "This looks delicious," Marcus said, but waited for the women to eat before he did. Unlike her father, who simply tucked in.

The conversation over coffee was more congenial. Talk of the weather, economics in Crystal Springs, and new arrivals in town, including babies.

Molly rolled her eyes. Of course, Father would bring the conversation back to her marrying. Sooner than later, if he had his way. It wasn't that he wanted to rid himself of her. The way he explained it, he was saving her from the embarrassment of becoming a mail-order bride when she couldn't find a husband in spinsterhood.

Besides, he wanted to vet her husband-to-be, and that would be difficult if the only information was via correspondence. How would they know the potential groom was telling the truth? She knew Father had her best interests at heart, but it didn't always seem that way.

"It's been a wonderful evening," Marcus said when her father stood, signaling their time was at an end.

"Thank you for joining us, Marcus. It's been an absolute pleasure," Father said, laying on the charm.

"The pleasure has been mine," Marcus said. "Eating alone is never fun."

He pulled out his wallet, and Father objected. "Tonight is on me," he said, reaching for the bill.

"Not this time," Marcus said firmly. "I must insist. I've had a wonderful evening—it is far from what I expected." He glanced across at her as he said the words, and Molly felt the heat rise in her face. Father grinned. Was this what he planned all along?

Had he invited Marcus to join them with intent? Bringing the pair together would certainly make her father happy, especially if it ended in marriage. But would it make her happy? Or even Marcus? She truly wasn't sure. For now, she would go along with her father, but if things looked like they were becoming serious, she would pull back. If that happened, she would have to speak seriously with the doctor.

Marcus handed over a chunk of notes, then opened the door for the others to go ahead. He walked with them until they reached the buggy they'd come to town in. It wasn't terribly far, but it was too far to walk home. Especially at night.

"Here we are," Father said, handing his wife up into the buggy. Without another word, he climbed up himself, leaving Marcus to hand Molly up. She could see what he was playing at—and he was being far from discreet. Molly felt like screaming, but the lady in her refrained. Perhaps later she could have words with her father, although she knew it was useless. He would take no notice of his only unmarried daughter.

"Let me help," Marcus said, a grin on his face. It was as though he saw right through Father. She was glad he did—that way, he might not be drawn into his shenanigans. He held Molly around the waist and helped her up onto the buggy. Father's eyes never left her and Marcus, but Mother ensured she looked forward.

"Thank you, Doctor Ryan," Molly said once she was settled.

"Please," he said, glancing up at her. "It's Marcus. Doctor Ryan is my work persona." He smiled, and a shiver ran from the top of her head to the tips of her toes. It was all Molly could do to not visibly shudder. Doing so would make her father extremely happy.

Molly wouldn't give him the satisfaction. Not tonight, anyway.

"Good night to you, Marcus," Father said, then flicked the reins to start the horses moving. "A good man, with excellent manners. Magnificent prospects, too."

"Father!" Molly said, exasperated. "What if Marcus heard you?" Her face was burning. Thank goodness it was too dark for anyone to see.

Mother reached over and held her hand. "He's a wonderful man," she said. "I'm certain he would make a good husband and father."

Her heart pounding, Molly looked away. Right this minute, she was too furious with both her parents to even answer. It did, however, make her think. Marcus was rather nice, and he was very handsome, as men go. She certainly wouldn't mind marrying someone like him.

The last thing she wanted was to marry a stranger. If it came down to it, Father may force her to marry someone by correspondence. Her heart pounded—but differently this time. Terror filled her. She would never marry a complete stranger. She would die before she allowed that.

Tears rolled down her cheeks. Thankfully, it was dark enough to hide her feelings and her tears. She felt some affection for the doctor, so perhaps it could become more?

Molly shook herself mentally. She didn't want to marry, and she would not allow her father to force her into it.

She kept silent the rest of the way home, no matter Father tried to pull her into conversation about the handsome doctor.

Chapter Seven

Marcus ambled home. After the heartwarming evening he'd spent with Molly and her family, he now felt completely alone. Joseph may have invited him to other family meals, but Marcus was certain he was only being polite. Why should he think otherwise?

Molly appeared quite uncomfortable much of the time. He glanced her way whenever he thought he could get away without her noticing. She was incredibly beautiful and had the most striking blue eyes. He knew he could get lost in those eyes. In fact, he almost had.

He'd had to concentrate on the conversation, otherwise he would miss far too much. And that would never do. Molly had been caught woolgathering a time or two. They all have moments like that, but he'd found himself doing it more and more this evening. The feeling of Molly in his arms this afternoon had never left his mind.

Why he'd done that, he didn't know. But she was so soft and pliable, and he was lost whenever she was around. It would be his undoing if he wasn't careful. Marcus was not interested in a relationship, and he certainly wasn't interested in marriage. As far as he was aware, neither was Molly. She seemed more like the independent type.

At least when she was working. She'd come across as far more demure this evening. There seemed to be two distinct sides to Molly Cavendish—the one her parents knew, and the persona she had at work. That wasn't necessarily a bad thing.

Marcus did the same thing himself. It kept him from being Doctor Ryan twenty-four hours a day and allowed him to be himself after hours.

He nodded. Good for Molly. A woman who knew what she wanted. He liked that. At least, he thought he did.

He watched as the buggy went out of sight. How he'd never met Molly before, he wasn't certain. He wasn't one to frequent the bakery, or the diner, for that matter. Rarely did he go anywhere, except to the mercantile. And now it was off his favorites list.

Dennis was infuriating not only to Marcus, but to most of the townsfolk. They only tolerated him because he owned the mercantile and they had little choice. It was at least an hour to the next town with a decent sized store. Time Marcus usually couldn't afford. Between his surgery and home visits, not to mention emergencies, he had little time to himself as it was.

Perhaps he needed to make the time. Particularly if he wanted to side-step Dennis. Although the run-in he'd had with Dennis today might make the other man stop and think.

Somehow, Marcus didn't think so.

The man was a pest. If the sheriff could legally run him out of town, Marcus was certain he would. He'd been interfering for far too long. From all accounts, it was longer than Marcus had been in town. The worst of it was Dennis was not married, and yet he proclaimed to know what was best for the unmarried men and women of Crystal Springs? If it hadn't been so frustrating, it would be laughable.

Marcus felt fury growing inside of him again. He stopped walking and stood outside the bakery. He had happy thoughts of being there this morning, and thought it might, perhaps, help him calm down.

He spotted the wooden bench close to the bakery and sat himself down. He tried some techniques he'd suggested to patients with anxiety. Breathing slowly in and out. Relaxing his body bit by bit. Closing his eyes and thinking about happy memories.

Feeling a little better, Marcus stood. He couldn't sit on this wooden bench all night. It was already past his regular bedtime.

The thought made him laugh. What sort of suitor would he be? Most nights, he was in bed not long after supper. Still, if he had a wife, perhaps his routine would change. He shook his head in the dark. Thank goodness no one was around to witness his antics.

Standing on shaky legs, he headed home. As he approached, Marcus stared into the darkness that was his home. For the first time, he didn't want to go inside. Not alone. Instead of wondering the reason, Marcus knew exactly the reason for his reluctance.

Miss Molly Cavendish. Not only had she turned his life upside down, she'd penetrated his heart. Something he believed would never happen.

Marcus awoke soon after the sun had risen.

After tossing and turning all night, he gave up. He put on his robe and slippers, then took himself to the small kitchen that was really only built for one. It was strange—there were enough bedrooms to accommodate several children, as well as husband and wife—but the kitchen was tiny.

He filled the kettle with water and placed it on the stove. Little heat emanated from the stove, so he began adding twigs and paper, getting it fired up again. It was his habit to fill the kettle and stoke the fire before bed each night, but his mind was in turmoil after last night's supper, and he'd forgotten.

He strolled into the bathroom and began bathing. This morning, he would use cold water to clean himself. It was no one's fault but his own. Taking the face cloth, Marcus washed his face, then the rest of himself. He dressed, then returned to the kitchen.

It looked like coffee was out of the question this morning. It was a lesson he wouldn't forget—coffee was his favorite way to start each morning. He pulled out his pocket watch and wondered if Molly would have arrived at the bakery yet.

It was a long shot, but she made great coffee. If she wasn't there yet, he'd have to endure Joel's awful coffee. Still, he had little choice.

He polished his boots, pulled them on, then headed outside. About to lock the front door, he halted. Since when did he polish his boots in the middle of the week? That was a task assigned to Sunday morning before church.

Marcus shook himself mentally. Then he rolled his shoulders. Was he acting foolishly? Because Joseph Cavendish had taken a liking to him, did not mean his daughter had. Of course, he wasn't going to the bakery to see Molly. He was going for coffee.

He pulled the front door closed and listened for the click of the lock. Then he strolled toward the bakery, whistling as he did so. His heart pounded. What was wrong with him?

Glancing toward the bakery, he saw Molly arrive. His heart fluttered, and he hurried toward her. It was for the coffee. That's all it was—he needed coffee.

Molly was standing behind the counter by the time Marcus strolled inside. He'd slowed his step to ensure he didn't arrive at the same time she did. He didn't want to appear too eager—that would never do.

"Good morning, Doctor Ryan," Molly said, a wide smile covering her face. "I had a wonderful time last night."

Did she? Molly hadn't seemed particularly happy at the diner, when he was forced upon her by her father. Dare he say her scheming father? "It was very nice," Marcus replied. "I rarely go to the diner, but when I do, I eat alone."

Molly suddenly appeared sad. "There's no need for that," she said. "We're all friends." Without him even asking, Molly poured him a mug of coffee. "Is that why you're here?" She smiled again, and his heart fluttered. Would he even be able to carry his coffee to a table? His shaky legs told him no, but his resolve told him he must.

"Thank you, yes. I forgot to stoke the fire last night." He shrugged then. "No hot water this morning."

Molly laughed. The tinkling sound sent shivers running down his spine. If he hadn't already felt unsteady, he certainly did now. Marcus knew it had been a mistake to come here this morning. If he hadn't been desperate for coffee, he would have stayed at home.

The unfortunate fact, no matter whether he wanted to believe it, was that Cupid's arrow had hit him right where it mattered—in the heart. How had he not noticed Molly Cavendish before? She'd been working at the bakery for quite some time, according to Joel. Before the twins were born, and they were what? At least ten months old. Perhaps even older.

He took a sip of Molly's delicious coffee. "You make the best coffee, Molly." He couldn't help but smile, and Molly threw a coy smile his way. The fluttering of his heart had become annoying.

She turned around and pulled out a small plate. "Something to eat? I'm guessing you haven't eaten yet."

Marcus surveyed the pastries in the glass display cabinet. "You guessed correctly. I'll take two—whatever you think is best." He smiled again. "Thank you, Molly."

Heat rose in her cheeks. She turned away again momentarily and replaced the smaller plate with a larger one. Stark white, which seemed to be the way of the bakery. At least from what he'd seen so far. Even the coffee mugs were white.

"I'll bring it over shortly. Sit down and relax." Molly leaned down into the display cabinet, adding two pastries to the plate.

Marcus stared as a wisp of hair became loose from the rest of her hair, which was pulled back in a severe style. It took all his resolve not to reach out and push it back to where it belonged.

He couldn't help himself—he watched her every move. The aroma of freshly cooked pastries permeated his senses. To distract himself, Marcus took another sip of coffee. If he was truthful with himself, it wasn't the aroma that had him distracted. It was Molly Cavendish. She might not be wearing the most beautiful gown—she wore her work clothes, and they were all but covered by a crisp white apron.

"Here you are, Doctor Ryan," she said, placing the plate in front of him. "Is there anything else you'd like?"

Marcus slid his hand toward hers, then stopped. What on earth was he doing? This time, his heart pounded. He was acting like a love-struck teenager, and it had to stop. He glanced up into her face. "Call me Marcus," he managed, hoping his voice would not deceive him.

Molly nodded. "Would you like me to put it on your account?"

"I'd rather pay. I promise not to leave my wallet behind today." He pulled out his wallet and handed Molly a wad of money.

She gave most of it back to him. "That's far too much, Marcus," she said, then turned back toward the counter.

Marcus no longer felt hungry. He could, however, sit and watch Molly all day. Instead, he brought one pastry to his mouth and took a bite. His taste buds were overjoyed. Joel was the best baker he'd ever come across. It was no wonder he sold out every day.

When he'd finished eating, Marcus pulled out his pocket watch. He still had time to go home and clean up before his first patient. Instead, he stood, intending to buy another coffee. Molly rushed over to him. "Is everything alright, Doc…Marcus?" His name on her lips sent a thrill through him.

"I'm more than alright," he said, resisting the urge to pull her close. "I have patients, so must leave," he said, when that wasn't what he wanted at all.

If he stayed, Marcus knew he would do something stupid, like invite Molly out to supper, or even worse, kiss her.

He dropped the mug back onto the table. "Thank you," he said, then rushed out of the bakery before he did something he could never take back.

Chapter Eight

Molly stared after Marcus. He was acting strangely. Come to think of it, he was like that last night, too. She didn't know what to make of it.

She shrugged her shoulders.

Molly glanced down to retrieve his soiled dishes. So much for his promise—Marcus' wallet sat in the middle of the table. The man was his own worst enemy. It was obvious he had a brilliant mind, otherwise he wouldn't be a doctor. It took a lot of brain power to learn everything a doctor needed to know. What she wouldn't give to be as smart as that. She shrugged again, then picked up the wallet and placed it in her pocket. Once again, Molly would have to pay Marcus Ryan a visit.

If he continued to forget his wallet, she would insist he start an account. At least that way he would only leave his wallet behind on the odd occasion when he paid his account.

The thought made her smile. Until it didn't.

Doctor Marcus Ryan rarely visited the bakery. He'd done it two days in a row so far, which meant he must have had a reason. He didn't seem like a man who normally skipped breakfast, and from all accounts, she was certain that was correct. What happened today to make him come to the bakery again? Surely it wasn't only the lack of boiling water for coffee?

Lifting his soiled dishes, she took them to the kitchen and placed them in the sink, ready to wash, then returned to the store and cleaned the table. She was about to turn away when the bell on the door tinkled. She knew who it was before she even glanced up.

"I did it again, didn't I?" he asked, a smirk on his face. Then he glanced down at the table and the wet cloth in her hand. "Tell me you found my wallet?"

Molly reached into her pocket and pulled out the doctor's wallet. He reached for it, and their hands met. Hers was wet and a little messy. His was warm and gentle. "Sorry," she said quickly. "I've been cleaning."

His fingers hooked around her hand. She glanced down. There was no sign he would release her hand any time soon. His wallet sat in his other hand. "Don't apologize," he said, his eyes staring into hers. "I'm the one who should apologize. Two days in a row is unforgivable." He must have realized he still held her hand because he suddenly let go. "I forgot to light the fire," he mumbled, which was totally confusing to Molly, although he mentioned something about the fire earlier. Her mind had unfortunately been in other places.

"The fire?" she repeated, having absolutely no idea what he meant.

He nodded briefly. "Last night—I forgot to light the fire. I mean the stove. I had no heat for the stove to make coffee." The man was tripping over his words. Molly had never seen him like this. Then again, she'd only met him yesterday, which was difficult to believe. It felt like they'd known each other forever.

She laughed then, and he smiled. "You can always come here for coffee. Next time, though, leave your wallet home. I'll make you an account."

"Agreed. But now I must be away. My clinic begins," he pulled out his pocket watch. "In about ten minutes. I don't like to keep patients waiting."

"Have a good day, Doctor Ryan."

He stared at her momentarily and opened his mouth to speak, but closed it again. Was he going to correct her for calling him doctor? She would never know because he spun away and left the bakery.

The store suddenly seemed cold and empty. Molly knew it was neither. Warmth from the ovens always filled the store. The clatter coming from the kitchen meant Joel was in his glee—cooking the day's produce, which was the thing he loved best.

Molly stared down at the empty table. The place where Marcus Ryan had sat a short time ago. She reached down and touched the chair he'd used. It was still warm. She sat down, promising herself it would only be for a moment. His warmth filled her. Molly didn't know what to make of it. She'd never felt like this before.

Never had she been distracted like this. She'd never given Joel the opportunity to complain about her work, or the fact she was not doing enough. Now she sat where the customers were meant to sit. She was staring into space instead of washing soiled dishes.

She had it bad. Molly knew she did. The easiest way to remedy the problem was to keep away from Doctor Marcus Ryan. If he came into the bakery again, she would send him away. Refuse to serve him.

The trouble was, she knew she couldn't refuse one of Joel's customers. Nor did she want to. Especially this one.

The rest of the day felt more like three days rolled into one. Molly couldn't settle back into her routine.

She dearly wanted to. She didn't like this feeling of wanting to see someone who was untouchable. After all, why would a man like Marcus Ryan, a doctor no less, be interested in someone like her who had been raised on a small farm?

Her father was not rich. He didn't have money to burn, but neither was he poor. There was always money for clothes, the farm was self sufficient, and she had never gone without. That didn't mean someone like Marcus Ryan would be interested in the likes of her.

Molly shook her head. Why was she even thinking that way? Marcus wasn't interested in her like that. She and her family were more like friends to him. Father knew him well, apparently. In what context, Molly had no idea.

At least that was the feeling she got from their supper last night. She still couldn't understand why Father had invited Marcus to join them. He had never been spontaneous. His decisions were always measured and well thought out. It was the reason his farm had always done so well. Selling to Dennis's mercantile as well as other store owners in the county kept him busy. The quality had always been high. Father had always been pedantic about that.

Molly finished drying the dishes and put them away. Joel had already left for the day. Once he'd finished baking each day, he left her alone.

Spending time with his young family was his favorite pastime.

It made Molly think about her future. She wondered what that would be like having children. Being a mother seemed a frightening prospect, but she loved children.

Would she and Marcus have children?

The thought hit her, hard. Molly did not know why she was even thinking that way. But of course she did—Marcus Ryan was a handsome man, and very special.

She finished putting away the dishes, ready for tomorrow, then headed out to the store. The bell tinkled, and she groaned. It was closing time. Besides, there was nothing for her to sell.

"We're closing," she called as she entered the store. "Oh!" she exclaimed, noticing it was Marcus standing at the counter.

He smiled tentatively. "I hope I'm not intruding. I only have a few minutes between patients."

Intruding? It was a welcome relief. She'd felt hollow all day, and now her heart was singing. It seemed so silly, but it was exactly how Molly felt. She did not know why that would be.

"I have nothing left to sell," she suddenly told him, waving her arms around the empty glass cabinets.

He grinned. "I didn't come for food. I came for you." His eyes seemed to twinkle, and she couldn't fathom why. "I can't stop thinking about you, Molly. Will you accompany me to the diner this evening?"

Molly blinked. More than once. Doctor Marcus Ryan wanted to take her to supper? Surely she'd heard wrong?

"You want to take me to supper?" she said, unwilling to believe she'd heard correctly.

He reached across and held her hand. "I do. Will you come?"

Her heart fluttered. His hand was warm and soft, and she never wanted him to let her go. "I…I can't," she said. "My family will be worried about where I am."

Marcus seemed deflated then. Suddenly, he brightened. "What if I get a message to them? Let them know you'll be with me. I'll ensure you get home safely."

He seemed so determined, and he had all the right answers. If he was willing to go to those sorts of lengths to take her out, who was she to say no? She didn't have to think about it any longer and smiled. "If you can do that, I can accompany you, only," she glanced down at her work clothes, "I can't go looking like this."

The smile that crossed his face suddenly disappeared. "You look beautiful to me," he whispered. "But if you feel uncomfortable, I'll take you home to change. It's not that far. Besides, the diner doesn't open for another two hours."

Her heart pounded. Could she? Should she? "I'll have to ask Father."

"Molly," Marcus said sternly. "You are a grown woman. Besides, I don't believe your father will object."

Molly hoped not. She liked Marcus Ryan, and it seemed like he liked her, too.

Chapter Nine

Marcus couldn't believe Molly had said yes. Albeit a little reluctantly at first, but she eventually got there.

Had he been foolish to invite her out so soon after they'd met? He wasn't convinced that was the case. She was a beautiful woman. She was also extremely pleasant and hardworking. If he didn't swoop in now, some other man may beat him to it.

"I have to go," he said, checking his pocket watch again. "I only have a couple more patients, then I'll be back. Will you be alright until then? You can sit in my waiting room if you'd like. It wouldn't be proper for you to be in my house. Tongues would wag, and we can't have that," he said, then winked.

She laughed. That enticing tinkle of hers almost had him staying. He would love the freedom of canceling his last patients, but they might truly need his attention. What if they were so ill they died, and it was his fault?

He reached out and held her hand momentarily, wishing it could be far longer. "You need to go," she said as she laughed. "Where should I meet you?" Then she shook her head. "No, I'll come to you—in the waiting room." She waved him away then, and he reluctantly let go of her hand, then moved toward the bakery entrance.

Marcus had never felt like this. He'd also never taken a woman to supper. Or courted.

He stopped in his tracks. Where did that last thought come from? Was he on route to court Molly Cavendish? What would her father say about that— if he brought the subject up?

It was far too early for Marcus to be thinking that way, but he worried about Joseph Cavendish's reaction. Although Molly was his last daughter to marry. Luck was certainly on his side in this case.

He unlocked the doctor's residence and went through to the bathroom. He felt disheveled. Unkempt. His demeanor seemed all out of sorts lately. He blamed Molly for that—she had left him feeling unlike himself.

Marcus knew he was not like other men in town. He had to be different. Always on alert, and always prepared to step in and help a sick or injured person at a moment's notice. The worst of it was he had no personal life. No time to think about women, about marrying, or even about having a family.

He glanced about his empty home. It was all good and well to provide the doctor with such a prestigious house, one with many bedrooms, but having no time to find a wife did not bode well.

Not that he was looking. Marcus stared at himself in the mirror. His hair was every which way. He needed to have it cut. His jacket wasn't sitting correctly, and his tie wasn't straight. He stared at himself in astonishment. What must Molly think of him, presenting himself to her in this state?

He adjusted his appearance and headed to his office. Marcus sat behind the desk for a minute, for what seemed like an hour, and tried to calm himself. He'd had quite a few days. Not difficult days, but different. He put his fingers to his wrist and checked his pulse—it was a little fast, but he could live with that.

Picking up the schedule for this afternoon, he went to the door and opened it. "Mrs. Periwinkle," he called, and the elderly woman stood. "It's been a while," he said, ushering her inside. He listened as she recounted her problems. He wished he were more attentive than he was right now. His mind was still on Molly Cavendish, and the way he felt when he held her hand.

Marcus opened the door after re-dressing Mr. Potter's infected hand, and there sat Molly.

His heart did a funny little skip. Marcus hated that he'd kept her waiting, but there was nothing he could do about it. In the future, he would ensure he was far more organized.

His mind suddenly froze. In the future? What if Molly decided she didn't like him and they never saw each other again? "I need to re-dress your hand again on Friday," he told Mr. Potter, then added him to the schedule. "Can you come at ten?" he asked and his patient nodded, and then was gone.

Only now did he dare glance toward Molly for more than a moment. She was smiling, and her cheeks suddenly turned pink. It was charming and very appealing. He walked over to her, then sat not far away. "I have to clean up in here, then we can go."

He stood, and then she stopped him. "I can help," she said, but he knew he must decline.

Marcus shook his head. "We can't give the gossips the chance to talk about us," he said. "I'll only be a couple of minutes. Then we'll go to the livery and arrange for a buggy."

She didn't appear happy, but nodded. "I understand," she whispered.

He hated the prospect of leaving her alone there, but had little choice. His footsteps seemed to echo as he walked back to his office to clean up. There would be no more patients today, and he left the office door open so Molly could see him, and he could see her. It didn't take long, and soon they were on their way to the livery.

Marcus helped Molly up into the buggy. His hands around her were almost his undoing, and he wanted to pull her closer and kiss her. He knew it was out of the question. Especially since her father knew nothing about his intentions. Not that he had any plans except to get to know Molly better. Once that happened, together they could talk about their future.

"Thank you, Marcus," she said. "I appreciate your help." His hands held hers, and it was clear he'd gone overboard with his attentions. The coy expression on her face was his first clue.

He hurried around to the other side of the buggy and climbed up. "How do you normally get home?" Marcus asked, not giving it a thought before now.

"Sometimes Father collects me, but most times, I ride home." She pointed toward one of the stalls. "That's my horse, Tilly."

"You were to ride today? Then we should take Tilly home with us." It was no problem, and in all likelihood, what Joseph Cavendish would expect him to do.

"I can ride her later—after supper," Molly explained.

"That is not happening," Marcus said firmly. "What if something happened to you on the way home? I'd never forgive myself." He climbed back down and, after preparing her and adding her saddle to the buggy, led Tilly to their buggy, attaching her behind. Marcus was no cowboy, but he knew one end of a horse from another. He was, after all, required to undertake house calls from time to time. "I believe we are ready to leave now," Marcus said, hoping he was correct.

"I do believe you are correct," Molly said, sounding nervous. Hopefully, her nerves were for her father's reaction to Marcus taking her to supper, and not from being in his company.

Marcus flicked the reins, and they were on their way. He'd been to their farm a time or two, but not for quite some time. As they drove along the stone-strewn road, he was thankful Molly finished work while it was still daylight. He hated to think of her riding along this road at night.

Trees and undergrowth shrouded both sides of the road. Anyone could jump out and attack at a moment's notice. He glanced about, hoping they were safe. He felt sure they were, but was ready to protect Molly at a moment's notice.

Arriving at the farmhouse, Mildred Cavendish came out onto the porch, still wearing her apron. More likely than not, she had expected Molly to be arriving alone, not having him tagging along. As Marcus brought the buggy to a stop, Mildred quickly turned and ran inside. When she returned, the apron was gone. He had to force himself not to smile.

"What's going on, Molly?" Mildred said, suddenly appearing distressed. "Are you ill?"

"No, Mother," Molly answered, amusement clear in her voice. "I'm perfectly fine. Is Father home?"

In some ways, Marcus hoped Joseph wasn't there, but knew it was only putting off the inevitable.

"He's in the barn with that new colt," Mildred said, curiosity creeping into her voice. "That horse is more trouble than it's worth."

Molly untethered Tilly, then led her into the barn. "I'll be back shortly," she called over her shoulder. Marcus knew he shouldn't, but couldn't help but watch her every movement, including the enticing sway of her hips.

When he turned back toward Mildred, she had a sly smile on her lips. "She's a good girl, Marcus," Mildred told him. "You could do far worse."

Her words surprised him, although they shouldn't. Mildred Cavendish was not a fool, far from it. He studied her closely. "I wish to take Molly to supper, nothing more," he said firmly, ensuring the mother didn't think he was here to ask for her daughter's hand in marriage. If it hadn't been so terrifying, it might have been amusing.

Suddenly Joseph was storming toward him, his expression thunderous. If this was his reaction to Marcus's request, he might as well leave now. "Lucifer!" Joseph suddenly bellowed. "He is Satan!"

Marcus cringed. Was Joseph referring to him? It certainly seemed that way. No matter, he knew he had to stand up to Joseph Cavendish or risk losing Molly. "Joseph," he said firmly, thrusting his hand toward the other man. When he glanced down, Joseph's hand was covered in blood.

"Dang horse bit me," he said, holding a cloth against his hand. Blood was seeping through. Marcus clamped his hand around the bloodied cloth in an effort to stem the flow of blood.

"Tilly? She seemed rather gentle." It was obvious Joseph was seriously injured, but Marcus didn't want to incite panic in anyone.

"Not Tilly, that dang colt I bought last week." Marcus stared at the blood still seeping through Joseph's hand. "I'm trying to break him, but he's having none of it. I've decided to call him Lucifer."

Marcus let out a sigh of relief. It wasn't him Joseph was calling Lucifer, but the horse. "Let me look," Marcus said. He turned to Mildred then. "Do you have medical supplies? Of course you do," he said, shaking his head. Molly ran into the house and soon returned with a large box. "I'll need some warm water as well," Marcus told her.

They moved onto the porch, and the two men sat, a small table between them. Marcus rummaged through the medical box until he found what he needed. "You have a well-supplied kit here," he said as he cleaned the blood from Joseph's hand. "I'm pleased to see you have a small bottle of carbolic acid. That should stop any infection." While Marcus did what he did best, Joseph glanced across at Molly. Marcus did not miss his smile. Perhaps now was the right time to bring up supper with his daughter?

"I hear you want to take Molly to supper," Joseph suddenly said. He was still smiling, so that put Marcus more at ease.

"It's the reason I came out to see you. But perhaps tonight is not the best timing given your injury."

"Absolute nonsense!" Joseph almost bellowed. "You've worked your magic. The bleeding has stopped. I see no reason for you to cancel. Is there?" He frowned then, and Marcus was quick to reassure.

"None whatsoever. I wanted to ensure you were happy with the arrangement." As he bandaged Joseph's hand, he let out a long pent-up breath.

"Anytime you want to take my daughter out, I am happy for you to do so." Suddenly, he stared into Marcus's eyes. "Should I be asking for your intentions? Oh, I know Molly is an adult, but she's still my little girl," Joseph said, emotion heavy in his voice.

Glancing up and meeting his eyes, Marcus did his best to again reassure Molly's father. "My intentions are honorable. Molly and I need to get to know each other better before we make any decisions about the future," Marcus said, then wondered if he'd already all but signed their marriage certificate.

Chapter Ten

Molly watched, terrified, as Marcus looked over her father's injury. The colt was young and frisky. And far too difficult for her liking. Of course, Father had broken many horses over the years, but this one was far more determined than any they had ever bought before.

Her heart pounded, wondering about the damage to her father's hand, but Marcus worked calmly and efficiently. He cleaned the wound with the supplies she'd given him and did so with care and affection.

Mother glanced her way a time or two, and Molly put an arm around her shoulder, trying to reassure her mother. Tears pooled in Mother's eyes. Mildred Cavendish was not one to give in to her emotions easily, but when it came to her husband, it was a different story entirely.

"We should make coffee for the men," Molly whispered, although they were far enough away the men wouldn't hear.

Mother glanced at her, then pulled away. "Of course. I have fresh cake as well." She hurried up the steps and inside the house, busying herself in the kitchen.

It wasn't long before Marcus and Joseph went inside. "Coffee for you, Father, and you too, Marcus." Molly placed a mug in front of them both, and Mildred added slices of the pound cake she'd made that very morning.

Marcus glanced at her. "Are we still going out?" he asked Molly, sending her a worried look.

"Given the circumstances, I think we should go another time." It saddened her, not only because she was looking forward to it, but because perhaps it would put Marcus off asking again.

"I've already told Marcus you must still go. I will not be the reason for either of you to miss out. Now change out of that dreary work gown," Joseph commanded, then reached for a slice of cake.

Molly stared at Marcus, who grinned. She wasn't sure if it was because of the cake, or the fact her father had expressed his approval. Either way, warmth filled her.

She ran possibilities for her attire this evening through her mind. What would be suitable for supper with a gentleman? One who apparently liked you enough to seek permission from your father to take you to the diner?

She heard footsteps behind her. Molly glanced over her shoulder to see Mother following her. "The sapphire blue dress," Mother whispered. "It matches your eyes."

It truly did, but was it too much for the diner? Regardless, Mother removed the gown from the closet and laid it carefully on the bed. She reached for Molly's best bonnet and set it alongside the gown. "Now all you need is your best boots," she said, then pulled Molly into a hug. "He's a good man, Molly," Mother told her. "And you're a good woman. You are lucky to have each other."

Molly rolled her eyes. "We only met recently," she said. "It's not like we are contemplating marriage."

Her mother pushed Molly away and stared into her face. "Do not dismiss his intentions. A man like that is hard to come by."

It was all Molly could do not to laugh. For her, this was a chance to get to know Marcus a little better. She was certain it was the same for him. It was a sad fact her parents, especially Father, had tried to marry her off for years. Molly had never been interested. Until now.

She promised herself not to get her hopes up. Things may not turn out the way she wanted. Or the way her parents intended.

"Hurry," Mother said. "Don't keep your young man waiting!"

Molly stared at her. Neither Marcus nor Molly were young, and she was certain Marcus was happily drinking coffee and eating cake. Then again, he was probably being grilled by her father. She sighed. Perhaps she did need to make haste.

"Thank you for attending to Father's injury," Molly said once they were on the way back to Crystal Springs. "I don't know what we would have done if you hadn't been there."

He turned to face her. "Any time," he said, then screwed up his face. "That didn't come out the way I meant. I truly hope Joseph does not need my help again."

"I know what you meant," she said quickly. "I appreciate your help, and I know my parents do, too." She slid slightly further away from him on the seat, not wanting to appear too forward.

"You look beautiful in that dress," Marcus said, then frowned. "Not that you didn't look beautiful before. Anything you wear is lovely."

Molly knew it wasn't true. Joel preferred she wore plain gowns, and certainly not colorful. He didn't want her distracting customers from the product. She completely understood his reasoning.

Soon they pulled into the livery, and he helped her down from the buggy. Molly's heart did a pitter patter in anticipation of Marcus's hands around her waist. When he'd done so as they left, he seemed— reserved. It was as though he felt awkward around her. Or perhaps it was because he was touching her.

There were far too many rules about propriety, and it put her on edge. It likely did the same to Marcus.

He pulled the buggy to the side and climbed down, then hurried around to her side. Extending his arms, he stared at her, as though he was seeing her for the first time. It was certainly the first time he'd seen her dressed in this fashion. She was wearing her best outfit tonight, for this special occasion. Her mother had seen to that.

Molly stood, then climbed down. Marcus held her around the waist. He stared into her face, focusing on her eyes. "You have beautiful eyes," he whispered.

Her mouth was suddenly dry. Marcus held her there for what seemed like hours, but was only minutes. Everything and everyone around them ceased to exist, and she focused on the man helping down from the buggy.

Then everything changed. The livery owner approached, speaking to Marcus as he did. "You still want the rig again tonight, Doc? Thought you'd be back sooner." His gaze went from Marcus to Molly.

"There was an emergency out at the Cavendish farm," Marcus told him. "It held us up a bit." He reached into his pocket and handed the man a dollar bill. "For your trouble," he said. "We'll be back later."

He put an arm around Molly's waist and guided her toward the nearby diner. Marcus made her feel special, like she really mattered. She could certainly get used to that.

As they arrived back at the Cavendish farm, Marcus realized he hadn't felt so happy, or so relaxed, in a very long time. Molly was good for him. Really good.

She made him feel important, and he certainly tried to do the same for her. Meeting Molly had changed his life, in the best of ways. Prior to knowing her, his entire life was centered on his medical practice. There was little he did that didn't involve looking after his patients.

It was extremely hard to believe it had only been two days since they met. Wait. Was it really only two days? Marcus found that challenging to believe.

After supper, as they pulled up in front of the farmhouse, Joseph and Mildred met them at the top of the steps. The sun was setting, but there was still enough light to see them clearly. Joseph wore a huge grin, but Mildred was far more reserved. As she always was.

Looking to the future, Marcus wondered what they would be like as in-laws. He shook himself mentally. Did he really want to think like that?

"I had a wonderful time tonight, Marcus. Thank you for inviting me."

Molly's words brought him back to reality and had him smiling. "I did too. Thank you for coming," he said, then hurried down off the buggy to help her. Fully aware his every move was being watched by her parents, Marcus barely touched her. He noticed the disappointment on her face. It sent warmth soaring through him.

"I trust you enjoyed the evening," Joseph said as they climbed the steps.

Molly smiled as she glanced at Marcus. "We did," she told her father. "I am grateful to Marcus for inviting me."

"The food was delicious, but the company was even better," Marcus said, then wondered if he was being too forward. Especially with Joseph in earshot. "We must do it again." He watched for signs of annoyance from Joseph, but there were none. It seemed he truly did have Joseph's stamp of approval, and that made him happy.

"I should probably go before it gets too dark," he said.

"Please dine here with us tomorrow night," Joseph said firmly, making it sound more of a demand than a request. "We know little about you," he said, and Marcus's heartbeat hastened. What did that mean? Was he being vetted as a husband for Molly? Everything seemed to be happening far too quickly. Despite that, Marcus felt he couldn't say no.

"I would be delighted," he said instead. "I'll bring my medical bag and check that bite. I have an early finish tomorrow, so I can bring Molly back home." He turned to her then and noticed Molly smiling. Why did merely glancing in her direction make him feel good? He wanted to pull her into his arms and kiss her, but he knew that wasn't possible. Not only because her father was standing close by, but because it simply wasn't acceptable.

If they were courting, it would be a different thing entirely. He wondered if that would even happen. Did Molly like him enough to let him court her? He already had Joseph's approval, so that wasn't a concern. Whether Molly saw him as merely a friend, or something more—that was the question.

Marcus turned to Mildred then. "What can I bring to contribute to the meal?"

Her face brightened, and she reached out and touched his shoulder. "That is very kind, but your company is all we require."

"Then I shall depart." Marcus turned to Molly and bid her goodnight, then climbed down the few steps to the buggy. "Goodnight, all," he said, then was on his way back to Crystal Springs.

Marcus ducked his head around the bakery door. "Good morning," he said with joy in his heart. Molly stood smiling behind the counter. "I've come for breakfast. It's far better than anything I can conjure up." It wasn't a lie. His coffee was terrible, and he was sick of baked beans and sausages most mornings.

He seemed to reach the counter in record time. "How did you sleep?" he asked Molly, reaching for her hand. She glanced down, but didn't object, so he continued to cover her hand with his.

"I slept well. And you?" He knew she was making small talk, but didn't care. Any time spent with Molly was time well spent. "You look better today. No dark circles…" Suddenly, she slapped a hand to her mouth. "I'm sorry. I didn't mean anything by it." She looked mortified, but he was quick to reassure her.

"Molly," Marcus said firmly. "I would rather you speak your mind. You are correct. I feel far more refreshed today. Perhaps dining with a beautiful woman is what I needed." He watched as color crept into her face. Once again, he found it alluring. He suddenly pulled out his pocket watch. "I suppose I should eat. My patients don't like to be kept waiting." He squeezed her hand. "However, I'd rather spend my time with you."

She suddenly pulled her hand out from under his and turned away. "Sit down while I get your breakfast," she said, and he was left in her wake with no choice but to do as he was told.

"The coffee was delicious, as always. As were the pastries." Marcus wiped his lips with a napkin, and Molly stared at his face. He lifted the napkin again, and she giggled as he put it down again. What was so funny? Suddenly she slapped her hands to her face, just as she had earlier. He gazed at her. "Is there something wrong?"

Instead of answering, she lifted her hand. Reaching for the napkin, she moved toward him, finally wiping at his beard. "You had some crumbs there," she said with a knowing smile.

Marcus reached up and grabbed her hand, and Molly dropped the napkin. With his heart pounding, he cradled her hand against his cheek. She stared at him with sad eyes. He let her go. Was she sad because he really shouldn't be doing that, or was there some other reason he wasn't aware of? Perhaps her father had changed his mind about Marcus?

Whatever the reason, it was worrying.

"I should get back to work," Molly said, snatching up his soiled plates. "I'll see you later." He nodded, but didn't trust himself to speak. What if Molly had changed her mind about him? She frowned then. "You are still coming tonight, aren't you?"

She looked deflated, so he was quick to reassure her. "Of course. Unless you don't want me to." Whatever made him say those words, he did not know, but now they were out and he couldn't take them back.

"Why would you think that? We're all looking forward to it. Especially Father. He likes you." Molly smiled briefly, then headed to the kitchen to wash his soiled dishes.

Marcus stood, her words running through his mind. He didn't want Joseph to like him more than Molly did. There was no point in that. It was early days in their friendship, he understood that, but he still needed for both of them to like the other equally.

On his way back to his office, he pondered the situation. Was he making far too much of her words? Or was this all one-sided? Marcus hoped he was wrong. He truly did. Molly had gotten under his skin far too quickly. Perhaps after tonight's supper, since he'd already made a commitment, he should stay away from Molly for a few days. Or even a week.

Maybe then, they would both know more about how they feel about each other.

His heart heavy, Marcus headed in to see his first patient.

Chapter

Twelve

Molly sat in the waiting room. The last patient was in with Marcus now. She couldn't wait to see him again. Her heart fluttered at the very thought of it.

Suddenly, the door opened and he stood in the doorway, staring across the room. He grinned when he saw her, and her heart rate kicked up a notch. What was it about this man that made her feel so…excited? Whenever they were together, he made her feel special, important. But Molly knew that wasn't the reason she felt this way.

Perhaps she should speak with her mother. They'd never really talked about men or marriage. Her sister was rather secretive about it, too. Living on a farm, Molly understood how babies were made, so maybe it was the reason Mother had never counseled her on such things.

"I'll only be a minute," Marcus said. His words startled her, and she jumped. He was next to her in a flash. He put an arm around her, then suddenly dropped it and stood. "I didn't mean to startle you," he said, then studied her.

She shook her head. "I wasn't paying attention," she told him. "It's fine. You do whatever you need to do."

He went back into his office, leaving the door open as he'd done another time. When he reappeared, Marcus carried his medical bag. "I have all the supplies I'll need to tend to Joseph's hand. I hope it's not giving him too much trouble," he said, then led her out of the waiting room and onto the street. Marcus locked the door behind them. "I have the buggy arranged, so we shouldn't be delayed today."

Molly's mind went back to yesterday, when Marcus lifted her into the buggy. The feel of his hands was still with her. A shiver went down her spine at the mere thought of it. "Mother was preparing a roast when I left this morning." She was trying to distract herself from her wanton thoughts, and hoped he didn't realize. "Mother is an excellent cook."

Marcus frowned. "I hope she didn't go to a lot of trouble for me. I wouldn't like that at all."

His words confused Molly. Why wouldn't her family treat him special? He was worth the added attention, although it didn't sound as though he thought so. "My parents both like you, Marcus. As do I." Surely Marcus wasn't insecure about his position in life? Or about whether or not people liked him. According to her father, he had a brilliant mind. He had to, didn't he, to become a doctor? One would think so anyway.

Except he seemed, well, socially awkward. Marcus didn't seem to be used to dealing with people who weren't patients. Except her. Oh, and Father. He seemed to connect well with her father. Possibly because he knew him already? Not well, but they were familiar with each other.

She really wanted to get to know Marcus better. If it turned out they were only friends, she would accept it, but she truly wished for far more. Doctor Marcus Ryan was handsome. He was a kind man, a gentle man, and seemed to be very caring of those around him. Molly didn't know how old Marcus was, but he had to be older than her, and she guessed at least thirty-two.

"Have you never been married?" she blurted out and immediately regretted not thinking first.

"What?" Marcus laughed then. "Never. Training to be a doctor takes years. There is no time for women. Then you need to establish yourself." He chuckled, then turned to Molly. "What about you?"

She stopped in her tracks. "I've never been married. Why would you even think that?" She was suddenly affronted, and realized she'd probably done the same to him. "I apologize," she said, feeling truly bad for speaking without thinking. Mother had often admonished her for this very thing.

He laughed, and she enjoyed the deep baritone of his voice. "I was only joking with you," he said, his smile suddenly gone. At that very moment, they arrived at the livery. Marcus placed his medical bag on the buggy, then helped her up. This time, his hands didn't linger, and he didn't pause to stare into her face. He was very business-like, and it bothered her.

If Molly was truthful with herself, it was devastating. What had happened between last night and now?

"The meal was delicious," Marcus said, rubbing a hand across his belly. "Not that I expected otherwise." He leaned back in his chair, a satisfied look on his face. Molly wondered how long it had been since he'd had a decent home-cooked meal.

He didn't seem the type to cook much for himself. She hated the thought he might live on canned food. Surely not? As a doctor, he would not condone anyone eating canned food regularly.

He pushed his empty dessert bowl away from himself. "That must be the best cherry cobbler I've ever eaten," he continued.

"How often do you cook for yourself?" Mildred asked. "I know some bachelors live on baked beans." Molly watched as her mother resisted the urge to pull a face. She might do so when it was the three of them, but not in front of company.

Red tinged Marcus's cheeks. "You got me there. I don't cook for myself much. I go to the diner occasionally."

Joseph raised his eyebrows. "My boy, you and I need to talk." He stood then. "The ladies will arrange coffee in the sitting room for us. We can talk while they clean up."

Molly was fuming. Both she and her mother were being pushed aside like they didn't matter. Besides, were the men going to talk about her? She opened her mouth to object, but her father threw her a stern look. Molly promptly closed her mouth again. She knew better than to defy her father.

She watched as the pair headed into the sitting room, then helped her mother clear the table. She made coffee and carried it to the sitting room. Marcus was tending to her father's injury. On her return to the kitchen, Molly poured boiling water over the soap in the sink, and watched it bubble, then scraped the dishes into the container they kept aside for the chickens. They always ate well.

Mother washed, and Molly dried. Normally she found drying dishes calming. But not tonight. "Settle down," Mother told her. "It's men talk. It's what they do."

"What you mean is Father is deciding my future. Not to mention putting Marcus on the spot." She pursed her lips in her fury, causing her mother to glare at her.

"That's not ladylike, Molly."

Molly shrugged her shoulders. "I'm sorry, Mother, I truly am. But it feels like Father is planning my life without asking me how I feel."

"I'm sure that's not it at all." Mother handed her yet another plate to dry. "Besides, what is there to plan? You've only known each other for a matter of days."

"Exactly," Molly said. She didn't add she would marry Marcus in a heartbeat.

With all the dishes now washed and dried, she replaced them in the cupboard. Molly removed the tablecloth and shook it outside, then wiped the table down and added a clean cloth to the table. She replaced the small vase of flowers her mother liked to have there when they weren't eating.

Then she headed into the sitting room, despite Mildred's objections. Molly stared at her father, who suddenly stopped talking. Marcus glanced up at her and smiled briefly, then stood. "Molly," he said, then waited for her to sit before he sat down again. It was clear to Molly her father watched his every move.

"What did I miss?" she asked, not caring what anyone thought. She glanced from one man to the other.

Father glanced at Marcus, then at Molly. "Nothing interesting. Marcus has checked my hand and re-bandaged it. It's going well," he said, glancing at Marcus again.

"It certainly is," Marcus said, smiling at Molly, but glancing sideways at her father. Why did Molly not believe either of them? She suspected more than ever they'd been discussing her. Or perhaps she and Marcus. Unfortunately, she may never know.

Marcus brought the mug to his lips and drank down the last of his coffee. Surely it must be cold by now. "Another one?" Molly asked, hoping he would stay a little longer.

He glanced outside. "I should go. The sun is beginning to set. I don't like the thought of driving home in the dark."

Mother walked into the room at the very moment. "It's creepy driving along that road at night. I don't blame you."

Father laughed at his wife's words, but said nothing. Marcus didn't respond, and it made Molly happy. She didn't like to think he would mock her mother. Or women in general.

"If you're determined to go," Father said, "Molly can see you out. Thank you for coming, and thank you for this," he said, lifting his injured hand. "I shall come in early next week, as suggested."

"Or perhaps Marcus could come to supper again and check it then," Molly said, wondering why her father hadn't already suggested it.

Father glanced at Marcus, who paled. It made Molly wonder exactly what they'd discussed. She would ask her father when Marcus left, but already knew he wouldn't tell her. A private discussion should be kept private, he would say. And he was right. Perhaps she wouldn't ask after all.

Chapter Thirteen

Marcus had a hollow feeling in his chest. His discussion with Joseph hurt, but had to be said. He liked Molly a lot, but wasn't certain she reciprocated in the same way he did. He was, after all, several years older than her, so perhaps their expectations were different.

Joseph understood his dilemma and supported him completely. They agreed he wouldn't see Molly for a week and reassess after that.

Marcus was regretting his decision. He'd left her less than twenty minutes ago and already felt the loss. It was difficult to believe he didn't even know Molly a few days ago. Yet he felt as though he'd known her forever.

If they both felt the same in a week, things might be different. The problem, as Marcus saw it, was he was rushing head-on into a relationship, when he'd never had one before. He'd flirted with a few women when he was at medical school—all the trainee doctors did—but that didn't mean he'd had a relationship. The longest time he'd spent on the same woman was a few days.

And therein was his concern. What if Molly Cavendish was just another opportunity to flirt?

He'd been honest and open with Joseph. As her father, he had agreed that Marcus should reflect on what Molly truly meant to him. It was natural he didn't want to see his daughter hurt. It was certainly not Marcus's intention, either.

As he drove along the quiet road, Marcus heard rustling amongst the trees. He'd heard stories about this road, and they weren't good. Stories of outlaws attacking travelers and robbing them. It put him on high alert. His horse suddenly shot forward, and Marcus flicked the reins. He glanced behind him, only to see a fox sitting in the middle of the road.

He let out a long breath. His heart pounded, and his immediate thought was of Molly. What if it had been a robber, and he'd been attacked? Or worse, killed? He would never see her again. The thought disturbed him.

But this wasn't about him not loving Molly—that much was clear to him, and he'd told her father. The issue for Marcus was he wasn't convinced she was as enamored with him as he was with her. He didn't want to marry Molly, or anyone for that matter, only to discover he was but a fleeting attraction.

"Molly, Molly, Molly," he whispered into the darkness. "How did I let you get under my skin so easily?" Marcus didn't know the answer to the question, but was relieved to see he was almost back at the livery. He drove inside and pulled on the brake, handing the livery owner a one-dollar bill for his trouble.

"Thanks, Doc," the man said, then unhitched the horse and led him to his usual stall.

Marcus strolled down the street toward home, but not before he stared at the bakery. He would miss going there each morning and seeing Molly. He wondered if she would miss him, too. That's what this week apart was all about.

He wanted to tell her, but Joseph thought it far better not to disclose their plan. His heart already ached, but his decision made, Marcus would not change his mind. How he would survive a week without Molly, he didn't know, but he would try.

~*~

Marcus stood outside his residence and stared down the street. Was he being foolish watching as Molly headed in to work? It took all his willpower not to run up the street to her and pull her close.

He knew he was doing the right thing, not only for himself, but also Molly. She needed to know her own mind. If she loved him, he would be ecstatic, but if what she felt was merely friendship, he would accept her decision.

Suddenly, he turned and went back inside. He poured himself a less than stellar mug of coffee and tried to drink it. The liquid was foul. Marcus much preferred Molly's coffee.

His toast was burned, and the baked beans were lukewarm. He wanted to shake himself. It was only day one, and already he was miserable. Would Molly miss him, Marcus wondered, or would she not even notice him gone? That was really the question, and the one he'd put to Joseph. If he truly meant little to her, what was the point?

To Marcus, she was an integral part of his life now, even after such a short time. Did she feel the same way about him? Marcus honestly didn't think so. It was the reason for his decision, and his discussion with her father. Joseph was a good man and wanted what was best for his daughter. As much as he wanted to see her married, like Marcus, he didn't want her to be miserable for the rest of her life.

After making himself presentable, Marcus went through to the medical clinic. He had paperwork to catch up on, so he might as well do it now. Perhaps his patients would be a much needed distraction? He truly hoped so. Otherwise, Marcus wasn't sure how he would get through the day.

It was not even half an hour later when Marcus heard a knock on the door. There was still plenty of time before the clinic opened, so he wasn't sure what was going on. If it was an emergency, they would pound, not knock gently as they did. He put aside the report he was working on and went to the door.

His heart pounded. Molly stood in front of him, a mug of coffee in her hands, along with a paper bag. "Good morning, Marcus," she said, a half smile on her face, despite the sadness in her eyes. "I brought these for you. I guessed you must be busy." Her arms outstretched, she handed him the items he had become accustomed to at the bakery each morning.

Marcus knew it was not the pastries, nor was it the coffee he went for. It was all about Molly. He stared down into her face. It was clear she was perplexed he'd not turned up this morning. "I have a lot of paperwork to catch up on," he said, knowing it was only a half truth. "I'm behind with reports, and that will never do."

She pushed the pastries into one of his hands and handed the coffee mug to him. "You can return the mug when you have the time," she said, then pivoted. Marcus could tell she was upset. It must have been difficult for her to come here. Did Joel put her up to it? The baker was far more astute than people gave him credit for.

He stared as Molly hurried down the street and back to the bakery. The sway of her hips was almost mesmerizing. How could he keep away from her for an entire week? He wanted to drive out to the Cavendish farm and take it all back. Tell Joseph he'd changed his mind and wanted to marry Molly right now.

Except Marcus knew it was not the right thing to do. Despite knowing he would love her until the day he died, he had to ensure it wasn't the wrong thing for her. He had to ensure Molly didn't make the biggest mistake of her life, even if that meant losing her.

Sitting back in his kitchen chair, Marcus savored the steaming hot coffee Molly had brought to him. He enjoyed the pastries, but not as much as he normally did at the bakery. He was fully aware it was no longer about the food, but it was all about Molly— the woman he wanted to spend the rest of his life with.

He knew he was doing the right thing. Joseph had confirmed it. He wouldn't have done such a thing if he thought it would be detrimental to his youngest daughter. Marcus knew he was correct. Knowing it was right didn't help his shattered heart. He simply wanted to curl up into a ball and climb back into bed. But that was impossible. He had a clinic this morning, at—he pulled out his pocket watch. In precisely fifteen minutes.

He stood and cleaned the crumbs from his kitchen table. This was exactly the reason he didn't eat at his office desk. Lifting the mug, he drank down the last of the aromatic coffee, Molly's wonderful coffee, then washed the mug with soap and boiling water. He would return it when he felt his heart could take it.

Hurrying to the bathroom, Marcus needed to check his beard. The feeling of Molly's fingers removing stray crumbs was implanted in his mind. Never again would he assume his face, or more specifically, his beard, was clean. She'd taught him that.

Staring at his reflection, Marcus knew he'd made the right decision, so why did his heart feel as though someone had smashed it with a sledgehammer? He noticed the dark circles under his eyes and splashed his face with stone cold water. It didn't help much. He only hoped his patients didn't notice.

He adjusted his jacket, more out of habit than anything, and ensured his tie was straight. He was a meticulous man. Marcus knew he was, but wasn't it better than being sloppy? His entire life played out meticulously. He learned the benefits of it while at medical school. Keeping sound patient records, ensuring supplies were well stocked, and keeping everything clean and tidy. He did all that. Until he met Molly, his life fitted in a perfectly sized container. Now he felt as though his life was in disarray.

For some strange reason, it hadn't bothered him. Until he exiled Molly from his life for an entire week.

Chapter

Fourteen

It was all Molly could do not to cry.

When she first met Marcus, she was smitten. She thought he was, too. He'd visited the bakery every morning, which he'd never done before, so she was certain it was because of her. Then, as luck would have it, he'd gone to the diner on the very night Molly, along with her parents, happened to be dining there.

Then he'd asked her out. The evening was enjoyable, to say the least.

She felt enamored with Marcus. It was as though she'd known him for many years, not mere days. Her mind went back to their last evening together—had she done something to upset him? Had her father frightened Marcus off? Although that seemed rather farfetched. For the past however many years, at least six, Father had been trying to marry her off. Now she had a viable suitor and suddenly he'd gone cold?

It didn't make sense. Something more sinister was afoot here, Molly was certain.

She stood behind the counter, tidying up after each customer had been in. There was little for her to do, for which Molly was thankful. Suddenly the bell tinkled, and she glanced toward the door, her heart pounding in anticipation of Marcus coming to return the mug she'd left earlier.

Instead, it was ten-year-old George Harper. He hurried toward the counter. When he lifted his hand, Molly recognized the mug she'd given Marcus, except it was previously filled with coffee. Now it was empty. And clean.

"Good morning, George," she said, her hand outstretched to take the mug. "Did Doctor Ryan send you to return the mug?"

The boy's face was beaming. "He gave me a whole dollar to bring it back. Said he was too busy." He handed over the mug, then dug into his pocket and showed her the dollar.

Molly's heart broke. Marcus had resorted to paying a child to come here, so he didn't have to face her. It told her far more than she wanted to know.

Marcus Ryan wasn't as smitten with her as she was with him. In fact, it seemed he now despised her. That much seemed obvious, since he didn't want to even look at her.

Only days ago, he told her how beautiful she looked, and fool she was, Molly believed him. Tears danced in her eyes, but she wouldn't let them fall. Especially not in front of young George. He might go back and tell Marcus, who might then feel sorry for her, and feel obligated to see her again.

She wouldn't have that on her conscience.

Tomorrow there would be no coffee for Marcus, and no pastries. He would have no need to send one of the local boys to return the mug. Hopefully that meant her heart would stay intact, and not feel like she would never find her soulmate.

How she got through the day, Molly didn't know. Joel knew something was wrong as he kept checking on her. His worried expression told her he was more than a little concerned.

Suddenly he stormed out of the bakery, his expression thunderous. The last time she'd seen someone look that way was when the new colt had bitten her father. Was that really only days ago? That meant it was only days since she'd enjoyed an evening with Marcus. And he'd tended to her father's injury.

It had endeared her to Marcus even more. He was a kind and caring man. So why was he treating her in such a shabby fashion now? There had to be a valid reason for his actions.

Molly stared as Joel stormed along the boardwalk toward the medical clinic, but she was certain that couldn't be right. Unless…had Joel injured himself and not told her? Perhaps she should close the bakery and follow him? Make sure he was alright?

She shook her head. Now she was being plain stupid. The last thing she wanted to do was show Marcus how desperate she was to see him. If he didn't want to see her, then she would not lower herself and become like some of those treacherous women she read about in the newspapers. Or in crime novels.

Molly was raised to be a genteel woman. Someone with manners and grace. Sometimes she had to fight her independence, but she knew when she wasn't wanted, and now she would take a step back.

She would not think about Doctor Marcus Ryan. Molly was determined to move onto greener pastures and get back to her happy self as she was before he came into her ordered life.

It hadn't been but ten minutes, and Joel returned. This time, his mood was a complete turnaround. The dark expression was gone, and now he was smiling. He entered the bakery whistling, which was not like Joel at all. He mostly kept to himself, and Molly couldn't recall him ever whistling before.

"Is everything alright, Joel?" she asked cautiously, watching his every move.

He glanced across at her and grinned. "Everything is perfect," he answered, then headed into the kitchen. Suddenly, he turned back. "Why don't you take the rest of the day off?"

"I…" Molly wasn't sure what to say. There was still another hour until she finished for the day. She glanced down at the glass cabinet. It was almost empty. One loaf of bread sat on the racks.

Suddenly Joel was bagging up the leftover bread, along with the handful of pastries. "Take these home to your family. You will still receive your full payment." He grinned again, then shooed her out of the store.

Molly pulled her apron over her head, more confused than ever. Something was going on, and from what she could tell, it involved both Joel and Marcus. And perhaps her?

What it could be, she may never know. Right now, though, her boss was sending her home with full pay. She'd be a fool to refuse.

Chapter Fifteen

Five days had passed, and from what Joel had told him, Molly was as miserable as Marcus was. He wasn't sure he could hold out another two days. His whole body ached from the pain of not seeing her, not hearing her voice, and not touching her.

He'd barely slept in those five days, and it was not good for his health, let alone his patients. Every day, Joel had visited during Marcus's lunch break to support him. To keep him on track with his mission. It had helped to listen to Joel talk about Molly and what was happening in her days.

But it wasn't the same as being with her.

Marcus still had half an hour before patients would arrive. It would be a little after that he would have to consult. Canceling was out of the question—his patients needed his expertise, and there was no getting out of it.

He glanced at his booking sheet, checking who he was seeing today. His eyes stopped when he saw Joseph Cavendish was on the list. Not only that, he was the first patient to be seen. Until now, he'd been sorely tempted to visit the bakery.

Or should he say, to visit Molly?

Perhaps Joseph would talk him out of it. Or would he do just the opposite? Marcus was undecided what to do, but settled on going to his office and catching up on the endless paperwork. It was the bane of his life, but for once, he thanked his lucky stars for the distraction.

Head down, he was finishing a report when he heard the waiting room door open. He checked his pocket watch—it was almost time to open, so he put the report aside and went out to greet Joseph.

Instead, he found Molly standing there.

She looked forlorn and distraught. "Molly," Marcus whispered. "I was expecting your father."

Molly stared down at the floor. "He got tied up, but asked me to let you know he will be here later today."

Marcus nodded, but wondered if this was a ruse by Joseph. Joel had told him repeatedly how upset

Molly had been, and perhaps this was Joseph's way of telling him too. "No matter. I'll fit him in when he arrives. His injury needs to be checked." His heart pounded as he turned away, about to head back into his office. He was certain Molly would leave. It had to be time for her to start work at the bakery.

With no movement behind him, Marcus turned back to face her. "Molly, I…"

She opened her mouth at the same time, her voice as full of emotion as his. "Why?" It was all she said before tears flooded her cheeks. It wouldn't be long before patients began arriving, so he ushered her into his office. This time, he closed the door.

His heart pounded. Marcus wasn't certain he could even articulate how he was feeling. The words he wanted to say rolled around in his mind, but whether he could say them was another thing entirely. Suddenly, those words all disappeared. Instead, he whispered, "I've missed you, Molly." He pulled her close and wrapped his arms around her, savoring every moment. Molly stood stiffly in his embrace.

Marcus wasn't sure if she was mad at him or annoyed that he'd taken such liberties, including closing the door when they were alone. It was something he knew went against every rule of propriety.

He glanced down and watched as she swiped at her tears. He leaned forward and kissed her forehead. He longed to kiss her lips, but not unless he heard the words he needed to hear. The affirmation that Molly was as smitten with him as he was with her. He longed to say those four words he'd rehearsed in his mind repeatedly.

Suddenly she glanced up at him, and relaxed. "I've missed you too," she said, sniffling. He pulled his handkerchief out of his pocket and handed it over. "Marcus," she whispered. "I don't know how to say this…"

His heart pounded. The truth was about to come out—she no longer liked him. "I love you, Marcus," she said, and his heart thudded. He felt lightheaded and thought his legs would go out from under him. "I was devastated when you abandoned me." Tears fell again, and he felt awful. He'd put the woman he loved through absolute hell, but Marcus was certain it was what he needed to do.

He pulled her closer and held her a little tighter. "I love you too, Molly. I needed to ensure you loved me, and it wasn't a passing phase."

Suddenly, her head shot up. Her fury was clear. "You did this on purpose? If you truly love me, why did you…?" She shook her head then and tried to pull out of his embrace. Marcus held her tight against him.

"I would not allow you to live a life of misery. If you didn't feel the same, I would have let you go. Despite being equally miserable as you have been."

She studied him then. "How did you know?" Suddenly, her eyes opened wide in astonishment. "Joel! He's been spying on me."

"All for the greater good."

Marcus heard the waiting room door open, then close. He needed more time with Molly. It was clear he would need to mend some broken fences. "Molly, I…" The door opened and closed again. He wanted to take his time. Now that Molly knew the truth, he wanted to wait a little longer. Instead, this was the right moment.

He dropped to one knee and glanced up at the woman he loved. "Molly," he said, his voice heavy with emotion. "Will you marry me?"

Molly studied him. Moments felt like hours. She brushed a stray tear from her face, then another. Marcus was sure he would keel over in fear if she said no. How would he live without the love of his life? He'd barely made it through five days.

"Marcus," she whispered. "I…" She closed her eyes momentarily. "Of course I'll marry you!"

He hurried to his feet and pulled her close. His heart still pounding, he lifted her chin, then kissed her gently.

The waiting room door opened and closed again. This time, far louder. Someone was getting impatient. "I hate to say this, but I must tend to my patients," he whispered, his regret clear, even to him. "I don't have a ring yet, but I will arrange for one sooner than later."

He brushed his thumb across her cheek, wiping the last of her tears away. "I do love you, Molly. I'm sorry, there was no other way to prove it." She nodded, and he hoped it meant she forgave him.

Marcus opened the door and stared at the few patients sitting there. Joseph was amongst them. Molly glared momentarily at her father, then her expression softened. Did she finally realize he had helped Marcus? He would ensure all the blame was on him and not Joseph. He would not be party to causing a rift in their relationship. She hurried out the door, no doubt heading for the bakery.

"Joseph," Marcus said, still feeling quite emotional. "Please come in."

Marcus sat behind his desk after closing the door, and Joseph sat opposite him. Marcus grinned. He couldn't help himself. "There's going to be a wedding," Marcus said, his voice still full of emotion.

Joseph's grin was huge. "Welcome to the family, Son," he said, then unwound the bandage on his hand.

The next four weeks went slowly, but now Marcus stood at the front of the beautiful Crystal Springs church. It was a place where he'd always found refuge, and felt at home in.

He stood nervously awaiting his bride, and now and then glanced back toward the entrance. This time, though, Molly appeared. With the sunlight behind her, she looked like an angel. Mildred fussed with her gown, then he watched in awe as Joseph hooked his arm through Molly's. Mildred then hurried down the aisle ahead of them. It made him smile.

Marcus would have opted for a quiet wedding in a heartbeat, but he owed it to Molly to give her the best day he could. He wanted it to be memorable for her. Suddenly the organ music began, and Joel elbowed him to turn toward their preacher, but Marcus didn't want to miss a moment of this wondrous day. The day Molly Cavendish would become his wife.

The moment Joseph and Molly stopped, not three steps behind him, Preacher Clyde Walters asked, "Who gives this woman to this man?"

With tears in his eyes, and pride on his face, Joseph answered, his voice heavy with emotion. "I do," he said, then offered Molly to Marcus.

Marcus couldn't believe this moment had finally arrived. Mildred had busied herself with the arrangements, especially the dress, which was kept a secret. From him, at least. Molly looked resplendent in her mother's wedding gown, the same gown Molly's sister had worn for her wedding. He knew the local dressmaker, Alice Goldie, had worked tirelessly to ensure the adjustments were ready in time for today's ceremony. He adored the fact Mildred's wedding gown could be used by both daughters for each of their weddings.

He gazed at Molly and grinned, then took her hands in his. He turned back the veil which had shrouded her face and took in her beauty. This scene had played out in his mind since the moment he asked her to marry him, and now it was a wish come true.

Marcus was almost convinced it was a dream. A dream he had prayed for with all his heart.

Epilogue

A year later…

Marcus sat in the sitting room with Joseph as they drank coffee. Molly sat close to him. He lifted a hand and touched her very swollen belly. "I think we should leave now," he said quietly. "You need to rest up before the baby comes."

Molly glanced at her parents sitting around the room. Her sister and her family had already left, along with her brothers, who had their own farms not far away. Marcus seemed determined, but she didn't feel up to leaving. "I'm exhausted," she whispered. "The baby has been active all day. Perhaps we can stay here tonight? I'm sure Mother and Father won't mind."

Mildred stood. "Of course not. There are fresh sheets on the bed already. Let me help you," she said.

Marcus's hand roamed over her stomach, then halted. "How long has the baby been doing this?"

he asked, his expression intense. He slid his hand to another spot, then paused, repeating this several times.

Molly gazed at him. "Several hours. Most of the day, I guess. Is something wrong?" She was suddenly concerned, but Marcus was here, and that was all the reassurance she needed.

Her husband glanced up at Mildred. "I'm going to need several towels. Joseph, I'll need my medical bag—it's in the buggy." Marcus stood, then helped a confused Molly to her feet. "You're in labor, my darling. The baby is coming."

Molly's heart pounded. The baby was coming? Now? "Are you certain?" She giggled then, and Molly knew it was her nerves.

Marcus stared down at her. "I'm certain. Let's get you laying down where you will be more comfortable." Marcus held one arm while Mildred held the other. Joseph hurried outside to fetch Marcus's medical bag.

"I thought I would have known," Molly said, tiredness overtaking her. Suddenly, she felt a whoosh. She looked down in astonishment at the puddle surrounding her. "I suppose that means you are right."

"Of course he's right," Joseph told her, handing Marcus his medical bag. "Your husband is the best doctor in the county."

Molly knew Father was right, but that didn't ease her concerns. She was about to birth a baby. Her brilliant, loving husband was about to deliver their baby, but she was still worried. Women died giving birth, along with their babies. She clutched Marcus's arm.

He turned to her and seemed to read her mind. "Everything will be alright," he whispered. "I'll be with you the entire time. No one is sending this husband out of the room." He laughed then, and his deep laugh lifted her spirits.

She turned to her mother, who was also smiling. "I'm going to be a grandmama," she said, and Molly knew it was all theatrics. Her family was trying to keep her calm.

Thankfully, it was working.

Marcus worked tirelessly, ensuring both mother and baby survived. It was a complicated birth, but several hours later, he handed their son to Mildred, who, with tears flooding her cheeks, wrapped her new grandson carefully, then handed him over to Molly.

As much as he wanted to go to Molly, to hold her and thank her for their miracle child and all she had endured, he still had work to do. From the worried look on her face, it was clear Mildred knew it was touch and go with the pair, but said nothing. Not to him, and certainly not to Molly.

Marcus would not put his wife through this again. There were ways to stop her from becoming pregnant, and he would ensure she had the best. Next time, he might lose her. He simply wouldn't take the risk.

Of course, he would talk to Molly about it before acting, but he was certain she would agree. They loved each other far too much and planned to spend the rest of their lives together. For Marcus, that meant they would grow old together. His plan didn't include becoming a widower in his thirties. He wanted her by his side until the day he died.

He watched as Molly's eyes fluttered closed. He checked all her vital signs. Felt her stomach, and ensured she wasn't hemorrhaging again. Praise the Lord—she was exhausted, that's all it was. He kneeled at her side and said a silent prayer, then took his son in his arms. Marcus had been far too concerned about his wife to even glance at the baby.

Now he stared into their son's face. He had the clearest skin, and striking blue eyes, just like Molly's. His hair was brown like hers and there was so much of it, more than he'd ever seen on a baby. He gently brought his son to his face and kissed his forehead.

They would choose a name for him later. Right now, though, Marcus once again silently prayed his thanks to God for this miracle. For keeping his wife safe, and for helping him bring his son safely into the world.

"I love you, Molly," he whispered. "More than you will ever know." Marcus heard footsteps behind him and glanced over his shoulder. Both Joseph and Mildred were there, both worried about their daughter while clearly ecstatic over the birth of their grandson. It was clear they had mixed feelings. "They are both fine," Marcus said, not recognizing his own voice. It was so thick with emotion.

"Thank you," Joseph said, emotion heavy in his voice, too. "Without you, neither would have survived." He took the baby from Marcus's arms and held him against his chest, then laid the as yet unnamed baby in the crib he had made for when Molly and Marcus visited.

Joseph then pulled Marcus into a hug, which also included Mildred. "We need to pray," he said after a few minutes of them all huddled together. "Dear Lord, thank you for keeping my family safe," Joseph said, still emotional but sounding far happier now. "And thank you for sending Marcus to us.

Without him, we would not have our Molly now. Amen."

For the first time, Marcus allowed himself to think about anything other than saving his wife and son. "Amen," he said, then broke down. Joseph held him close, and Marcus knew everything would be alright.

From the

Author

Thank you so much for reading my book – I hope you enjoyed it.

I would greatly appreciate you leaving a review where you purchased, even if it is only a one-liner. It helps to have my books more visible!

About the

Author

Multi-published, award-winning and bestselling author Cheryl Wright, former secretary, debt collector, account manager, writing coach, and shopping tour hostess, loves reading.

She writes both historical and contemporary western romance, as well as romantic suspense.

She lives in Melbourne, Australia, and is married with two adult children and has six grandchildren. When she's not writing, she can be found in her craft room making greeting cards.

Links

Website: *http://www.cheryl-wright.com/*

Facebook Reader Group:
https://www.facebook.com/groups/cherylwrightauthor/

Join My Newsletter:

https://cheryl-wright.com/newsletter/
(and receive a free book)